For my mum – KH

For my niece Yasmin – CC

STRIPES PUBLISHING
An imprint of Little Tiger Press
1 The Coda Centre, 189 Munster Road,
London SW6 6AW

A paperback original
First published in Great Britain in 2016
Text copyright © Kris Humphrey, 2016
Illustration copyright © Chellie Carroll, 2016
Map copyright © Artful Doodlers, 2016

ISBN: 978-1-84715-650-1

GATHERING VOICES

Kris Humphrey

Illustrated by Chellie Carroll

CHAPTER 1

Mika woke to the sound of the guard's boots. After seven days hiding below ground, she had grown used to that slow, tired thud on the stairs. It was a sound that meant morning had arrived.

She reached a hand out and felt Star, her arctic fox companion, curled beside her. Star seemed so small while she was asleep, a perfect ball of white fur. Mika stroked her gently, not wishing to wake her just yet.

Star had been out in the city during the night, scouting for food. She had found a rice cellar in an empty house nearby, which Mika and the others planned to raid for provisions that morning.

Mika let her hand rest on Star's thick fur and stared into the absolute darkness of the basement.

She wished she was above ground, tasting the crispness of the highland air. Outside, the sun would be creeping over the mountain peaks that surrounded the city of Rakeen – her home. The sky would be a brilliant blue, the same blue as the lakes that studded the hills and valleys beyond the city walls. The rooftops of Rakeen would be flecked with snow, which would soon melt and trickle melodiously through the city's network of streams and gutters.

Mika felt a pang of grief at the thought of how that would be the only sound in the streets of Rakeen. There would be no cooking fires crackling, no vendors touting their wares and no horse or cattle hooves clattering over the cobble stones.

The city was empty of people. Only demons walked there now.

They were called the Narlaw – shape-shifters who could take on the appearance of anyone they touched. And to be touched by a Narlaw meant falling into deep unconsciousness – the ghost-sleep. The demons were faster and stronger than any human. They consumed all living things, leaving a trail of ruined country in their wake.

This was not the first time the Narlaw had attacked the kingdom of Meridina. Every child knew about the first invasion, one hundred years ago, when the demons had been defeated and banished from the kingdom by Queen Amina.

Nobody had expected them to return.

But the Narlaw had attacked more swiftly this time and even Rakeen's fierce militia hadn't stood a chance. As far as Mika knew, she and the dozen or so others in the basement were the only survivors. Everyone else had been plunged into the ghost-sleep or had died defending the city.

Light bloomed at the far end of the basement as the guard lit the first of the storm lamps. Around the chamber people began to stir, muttering quietly as they woke. Mika sat up, but she didn't feel ready for the day ahead. The thought of the scavenging mission filled her with dread.

As a Whisperer it would be her job to watch for Narlaw, while the others gathered as much food as they could from the cellar Star had found. Only a Whisperer could see through a demon's shape-shifting disguise and only a Whisperer could banish a Narlaw back to the Darklands. But Mika had never really learned how to banish a demon. It had been part of her Whisperer training and she was good at entering the earth trance, which was the first step, but she had been completely unprepared for the invasion. And so had her mentor, Astor.

Mika felt a stab of sadness for Astor. She had been touched by the Narlaw and now she lay in another part of the basement complex alongside three militia warriors, deep in the ghost-sleep.

Now Mika was the only Whisperer left in Rakeen – perhaps the only one left in all of the western highlands. It was a dizzying thought. She wasn't a leader or a warrior. For her, being a Whisperer had always been about the special closeness to the earth. She loved to feel all the life around her: the tumbling mountain streams with their tiny, darting fish, the hawks that circled above the foothills and the crystalline flakes of snow as they drifted down from the sky. And most of all she loved to feel the four winds blowing. Astor had passed down the ancient knowledge to Mika, teaching her how to channel the winds' power and use it in the art of healing.

Although she was the only Whisperer in Rakeen, she wasn't alone – she had Star by her side. The bond they shared was more than just a way to communicate without speaking aloud – as long as Star was nearby, Mika could always feel the warmth of her presence. Mika still remembered the first time she had felt that presence – it was the very beginning of her Whisperer training. While the other children in her village had started school, Mika had gone with Astor, climbing a long, steep path that led to her mentor's cabin. Mika had been nervous, unsure what her life as a Whisperer would bring, and sad to leave the other village children behind. But when she had followed Astor into the timber-walled house, all of her fears had vanished. Curled on a fireside rug was Star. Their eyes met and Mika realized she could feel everything the little fox was feeling – the warmth of the fire, sleepiness mixed with a shy excitement.

"This is Star," Astor had told her. But Mika knew that already, the newly formed bond pulsing with thoughts and feelings. This was her companion. This was what it meant to be a Whisperer.

Now, after years of training, after moving to the city with Astor and the terror of the Narlaw invasion, Mika's bond with Star was stronger than ever.

She looked down at her companion's brilliant white fur and watched her chest rise and fall as she slept. Star was as crafty and playful as foxes came. Mika thought fondly of how Star had often sneaked off to chase crows or steal fish from the marketplace near the river while she studied with Astor. She worried that life in Rakeen had made her companion tame – too accustomed to people, to the food and warmth of the city. The city had made Mika soft, too. She had all but forgotten the hardship of her early life in the freezing hills to the north. She had absorbed herself in learning, in her attempts to master the four winds.

And now the demons were here and neither she nor Astor had been able to stop them.

The guard passed by, placing a storm lamp near the foot of Mika's makeshift bed. A few feet away Mika could see her best friend, Zabeh, push back the blankets from her face.

"Another beautiful morning," Mika said, gesturing to the low ceiling and damp walls of the basement.

Zabeh half smiled. "The sooner we leave this mildew-smelling hole, the better," she said.

Mika smiled back. "I think I've just about got used to the smell."

Zabeh laughed and shook her head. "I keep imagining I'm back in the village. I wake up thinking all I have to do is swim in the lake or dig snow holes – then I see these walls and smell the mildew and reality crashes back in on me."

"If we *were* back in the village," said Mika, "you'd have to get up and go to school. No swimming or messing about in the snow."

Zabeh shot Mika a wicked grin. "As if school ever stopped me having fun," she said.

This was true. Mika and Zabeh had grown up in the same small village in the hills and, from the very beginning of Mika's Whisperer training, Astor had frowned on Zabeh as a bad influence.

"Fun usually meant us both getting in trouble," said Mika.

"So you missed a few lessons with Astor," said Zabeh. "Don't pretend you didn't enjoy yourself."

Mika grinned. It was impossible to disagree with Zabeh on that point. Also, Zabeh had always stood up for her. When a few of the village children began taunting Mika for being different, for being a Whisperer, Zabeh had faced them down furiously, despite being outnumbered. Mika would forever be grateful for that, and for the fact that they had travelled to Rakeen at the same time – Mika to continue her training as a Whisperer and Zabeh as an apprentice in the city militia.

Now, instead of village bullies, they were fighting the Narlaw together.

Along with a few surviving militia warriors, Zabeh had tried to help Mika and Astor escape the city.

They had been summoned, like all of the kingdom's Whisperers, to a council of war at the capital city of Meridar. But the group had been ambushed as they tried to flee from Rakeen. A demon plunged Astor into the ghost-sleep and all they could do then was retreat, carrying Astor and the fallen warriors to the relative safety of the hidden basement. Seven nights later they were still in hiding.

"I'm beginning to wonder if we'll ever leave this place," Zabeh muttered as she rose to her feet.

Mika watched her friend closely, but chose not to respond. She knew how frustrated Zabeh had become, how she'd rather try to fight her way out of the city than stay in hiding.

It was Mika who had urged caution and the pair of them had argued several times over whether they should stay or go. But Mika knew for certain that they wouldn't last long out in the open. Not with just one inexperienced Whisperer for protection. Her Whisperer sense meant she could feel when a demon was coming, but she was yet to banish one. Every night she felt them moving around above ground and creeping like a sickness into her dreams. She wasn't ready to try another escape just yet.

By her side, Star finally began to wake. Her tail flicked against Mika's hand, as soft as a summer cloud. She stretched out, her tiny black nose wrinkling as she squeezed her eyes shut in a yawn.

I was dreaming, she whispered to Mika. The words arrived directly into Mika's mind. *We were back at home,* continued Star. *There was a fire in the brazier and Astor was grilling fish. She was letting me sit on her favourite red cushion and she was saving a whole mackerel for me.*

Mika watched as her companion began cleaning her tail with small, sharp flicks of her tongue. Grilled mackerel sounded wonderful to Mika, too, but this wasn't the time for daydreaming.

If we're lucky, she told Star, *we'll bring back some decent food from that merchant's house. You did well to find it last night.*

Star looked up and her black eyes shone in the lamplight. *I told you my explorations would come in handy one day.*

Explorations? said Mika. *Don't you mean sneaking about and getting into trouble?*

I found some food though, didn't I? Star resumed her tail cleaning.

You certainly did, said Mika. *Now all we have to do is fetch it.*

Most of the militia warriors were awake now, busy preparing for the coming mission. Mika rose to her feet and rolled her bedding. She'd been wearing the same clothes for a week and the dampness of the basement had infused them with a musty smell. She reached for her coat, which she'd been using as a pillow. As she unrolled it, she felt the ridged embroidery on its sleeves and shoulders. As well as the standard diamond patterning, Mika had earned one wind icon – the yellow curl of the mild south wind, which was stitched on to her coat's left wrist. Channelling the winds was a difficult skill to master, but with technique and concentration it was possible for a Whisperer to draw a great deal of healing power from them. In time, Mika had hoped to master all four winds, like Astor. But now, with the Narlaw ruling the highlands and Astor trapped in the ghost-sleep…?

Mika lifted the storm lamp from the floor and headed toward a dark doorway at the end of the chamber. She nodded to Zabeh as she passed.

Back soon, she whispered to Star.

They both knew where Mika was going.

The adjoining room was much smaller and full to the rafters with carefully stacked timber – a reminder that the owner of the basement, and the grand house above, had been a respected architect. The stacked timber was windfall – wood that had been brought down by nature. White juniper branches shone like bone in the lamplight, more precious than gold. They could be used only for the construction of wind shrines – the intricate, whistling structures that crowned many a hilltop across the western highlands.

Mika passed through into the next chamber and raised her lamp high to see the four ghost-sleepers. Three militia warriors and Astor. As Mika approached her mentor's bed, there was a scrape of hooves on stone. Suri, Astor's companion, stood to greet her, shuffling uncertainly and swinging her great, curled horns from side to side.

It was a sad thing to see this proud, long-horned mountain goat trapped beneath the ground, pining for her companion. Mika felt Suri's confusion and fear as she lay a gentle hand on the goat's forehead, whispering thoughts of calm and reassurance. Suri peered up at her with doleful eyes and Mika tried to imagine the pain of being separated, even though Astor was right by Suri's side.

We'll banish them all, Mika whispered to Suri, unsure if her meaning was understood. *Astor will come back to you, I promise.*

But she didn't know how they could ever defeat so many thousands of demons.

Mika leaned over her sleeping mentor and performed what had become her morning ritual – reaching out, braving the stomach-churning sickness to search for Astor's presence beneath the smothering grip of the ghost-sleep. She felt a dim glow, like a single distant star in an otherwise empty night. This was Astor, alive but unreachable.

Mika wished with all her might that she could bring Astor back. But the Narlaw's dark spell was an impassable wall between them. Mika stood for a few moments more, looking down at her mentor. Then she stepped away from the bedside, stroked Suri on her bristly chin and left.

When she returned to the main chamber, Mika found the scavenging party ready to leave. Zabeh and three of the warriors were dressed in loose, black trousers and black, padded jackets. They were well armed, Zabeh with her short sword and Guran, the leader of the group, with a spear tucked into the strapping across his back. Jen and Yukio fell in behind Guran, both with bows and arrows.

As usual, Mika felt young and cowardly in the presence of such warriors. But Zabeh smiled at her, as if they were still small children about to run out and play in the new spring blossoms. Mika smiled back.

"Are you ready to guide us, sister?" Guran said. He dipped his head in a swift, formal bow.

Mika nodded. "We'll do our best," she said, as Star scampered across the basement to join her.

Stay sharp, Mika whispered.

There's no fox sharper than me, Star replied.

Guran led his warriors toward the stairs and Mika followed.

CHAPTER 2

As Mika crept through the main door and out into the garden, the sky unfolded, vast and brilliant blue. The air was cold and fresh, and the mountain peaks gathered beyond the city like old friends. Guran signalled and the warriors spread into a defensive formation. The garden had been fed upon by demons, but there were still some plants left that could be used as cover – a long hedgerow stood above the ravaged lawn and a thick cluster of bamboo stalks had also survived. They were the remains of a garden that had taken many years to grow and only days to destroy.

Mika kneeled at the centre of the group with Star, scanning for demons. After so long in the basement, the intensity of the outside world was overwhelming to her Whisperer senses, but she forced herself to concentrate. The house was clear and so was the garden. Mika reached out further with her senses, over the high stone wall and into the streets and gardens beyond. Nothing. But she knew that if she pushed further, she would soon feel the tell-tale presence of the demons.

Anything? she asked Star.

Not yet. Star sniffed the air. Her eyes darted and her tail twitched.

Mika sensed her companion's anxiety through the bond, but there was excitement there, too. If only she could share it, Mika thought. But all Mika felt was fear.

She signalled the all-clear with a sharp nod to Guran, who then waved them on. Mika rose and moved low to the ground as Star scurried beside her.

They reached a small grove of ornamental bamboo and Guran slipped between the swaying stalks toward the high garden wall and the side gate. Mika probed the narrow alley beyond. It was deathly quiet. She felt the cobbles, smooth and ancient, and the tiny lilac poppies that sprouted from the outer face of the wall. She checked with Star then signalled again to Guran and he pressed his weight against the gate.

Across into the next garden and Mika and Star began to settle into a rhythm. They scanned, searching for demons and marking out a safe radius around the group. When they were both satisfied, the group moved on, ducking and climbing, pushing through foliage and darting alongside the stone and timber walls of the grand, vacant houses. Staying focused was a constant struggle. Every sudden sound and unseen movement sent a jolt of fear through Mika's chest. She found herself twitching nervously at the creaking of a tree in the wind or the drip of water from a gutter.

Finally, they crossed the wall into the garden of the silk merchant and Mika landed with a thud on soft earth. Star dropped silently to squat by her side.

The mansion stood to Mika's right. The slopes of its roof were decorated with carvings, as were the few wooden screen doors that had survived.

I'll take the west side, you take the south, she whispered to Star. She breathed deeply to steady her nerves then cast her senses out across the muddied lawn, feeling through the rockeries and around the lifeless pond and the sculpted hedgerows.

Clear, said Star.

Mika caught Guran's eye and nodded.

He turned to Zabeh and Jen, motioning them on, and the two of them raced from the cover of the trees toward a cellar hatch at the top of the garden.

Mika watched Zabeh move. She was as quick as Jen and ran with absolute focus, seemingly unfazed at being the youngest of the warriors. She and Jen reached the hatch and together they heaved the doors open. Jen vanished inside and Zabeh crouched at the entrance, one hand on the hilt of her sword. She surveyed the area with impressive calm.

Time stretched. Mika scanned the gardens and the mansion as best she could. At every breath she willed Jen to emerge with the precious supplies so they could get going, back to the safety of the basement.

There was a burst of noise on the opposite side

of the garden and Mika swung her gaze away from Zabeh. A large gang of crows flapped skywards from a grove of trees. Their raucous shrieks were like a riot in the quiet of the garden. Mika searched the trees for what had frightened the birds into flight, but she felt nothing.

It was then she heard Guran's sharp intake of breath. Mika turned back to the cellar hatch. Zabeh had drawn her sword.

Mika followed her friend's gaze, out toward the rockery just a few paces from the hatch. She felt it then, a darting movement, a cold, sickening touch at the edge of her mind.

Mika cried aloud as the demon broke cover, its grey eyes glowing in the stolen face of a smart, portly man.

Guran was already running. Yukio unleashed an arrow, which barely missed Guran as it arced across the garden. The demon leaped at Zabeh just as the arrow hit with a horrible thump.

But the demon barely faltered. It fell upon Zabeh, knocking her sword away and pushing her into the dirt.

Guran howled a battle cry and swung his spear. He collided with the demon, slashing with fearless strength.

Mika stood, fixed to the spot. She had to banish the demon, but when she tried to enter the earth trance it slipped her grasp. The trance required calm, an all-encompassing connection to the earth that was tricky to maintain. Mika was too scared, too shocked by what was happening to concentrate.

Zabeh was on the ground, unmoving.

The Narlaw dealt a savage blow and Guran flew back. His spear clattered away as he landed. The demon looked up then, grey eyes meeting Mika's from across the garden. Another arrow flew and the Narlaw ducked away.

Mika closed her eyes. She remembered Astor and their long days of training together. She brought calm into her mind and reached down into the living soil. The earth trance came. A tide of warmth filled her mind and body – the earth's power, a tiny fraction of it. Mika knew what she had to do next.

She reached out to embrace the demon, but its presence touched her like poison and her concentration faltered. For an instant she felt the demon's fear. It knew she was a Whisperer, that she could send it back to the Darklands. But Mika's sense of calm was broken. She struggled desperately to maintain the trance. She had to do this. Zabeh needed her.

Mika cried out in pure frustration as the earth trance slipped away completely. She opened her eyes and saw Zabeh on the ground, the three warriors climbing to their feet as the demon fled from the garden in an unnatural blur of limbs.

Mika ran across the garden and dropped to her knees beside her friend. Star arrived at her side an instant later.

Is she all right? asked Star.

Mika couldn't speak. She couldn't even whisper.

Zabeh's eyes were closed. She was lost in the ghost-sleep.

They hurried back to their basement hiding place. Mika led the way, her mind racing with disbelief and guilt. Why hadn't she spotted the demon? Why couldn't she have banished it when she had the chance? Yukio carried Zabeh over his shoulder and Guran and Jen struggled behind them with two sacks of rice each. Guran was badly winded and limping from the fight.

Once they were inside the grand house where they had taken shelter, Guran gave the secret knock on the basement door and they were let back in. Yukio lay Zabeh gently on to a bedroll and Mika immediately kneeled at her side.

She clenched her eyes shut against the tears, her failure stinging in her chest. She felt a sudden fury at the demons. What right did they have to take her friend from her?

Star brushed up against her. *Mika,* she whispered. *It's not your fault.*

It is my fault, said Mika. *I didn't protect her. I didn't banish the demon. It was the only thing I had to do and I didn't do it.*

She reached out to Zabeh with her Whisperer sense, delving to feel the far-away glimmer of her friend's life. The dark of the ghost-sleep blocked her way. Zabeh was still there, but Mika could barely feel her at all. She knew it would do no good, but she reached down toward Zabeh again and again, each time letting her anger drive her as she clashed against the sickening demon presence that was holding Zabeh under its spell.

She pushed again, harder, more desperate than before. Her senses recoiled, and she felt Star shudder beside her as the sickness spiked across the bond between them. But Mika kept going, punishing herself for having let this happen and wishing beyond anything she had ever wished for that Zabeh would return to her.

Please, said Star. *You can't do anything now. We have to find the demon that did this and banish it. That's the only way.*

Find the demon? Mika whispered. *How do we find one demon in a city of thousands? How do we banish it when I don't even know how?*

31

Frustration boiled through Mika as she threw herself at the wall in her friend's mind. It was almost more than she could stand. But as she reached desperately for Zabeh she felt new sensations there – thread-like textures, sticky and yet tough, like spider silk. She flinched once again, but an idea had lit in her mind. She breathed deeply and slowly, letting calm settle over her. Then she entered the earth trance and the basement melted away around her. She no longer felt or heard Star, instead directing everything she had at the barrier between her and Zabeh.

She reached further and further, until the weave of the demon's binding became clear. Her trance had become deep now, and she felt the power of the earth swell through her. Mika grasped a strand of the binding as she had been taught to grasp a demon's presence during banishment. It snapped instantly.

Again and again she grasped and tore away at the binding, fighting her way into the sickening dark. In her head she chanted Zabeh's name, begging the earth for greater power, channelling it against the demon's evil.

She burrowed, destroyed and cleansed. The need to save her friend gave Mika more power than she ever knew she had. Finally a flicker of warmth appeared – Zabeh was within reach.

"Zabeh," she murmured aloud.

She could feel the threads of the demon's power coiling around her, sticking to her as she was freeing Zabeh of them. This was dangerous, but the realization couldn't stop her. She struck at the binding, tearing at it shred by shred. It was a never-ending web covering and confusing everything.

As Mika fought against the demon's power, she began to tire. She'd never maintained a trance for so long before, or with such intensity. She felt dizzy and weak, but she kept up her attack, and the web of ghost-sleep slowly dissolved before her.

As Zabeh's presence grew stronger, Mika drew strength from it. But then her head began to spin and a cry flew from her lips.

Her eyes snapped open and the room swung

around her. The floor leaped up and struck her painfully. For an instant Star's face was close to hers.

Mika blinked and tried to speak, but everything faded to black.

When Mika woke it seemed like hours had passed, but from the commotion around her she knew her faint hadn't lasted long. Guran crouched over her, a disbelieving grin lighting his tired face.

"Mika," he called. "Mika. Look what you did."

Mika sat up. Her head swam as she turned. She felt Star's damp nose on her cheek, followed by the roughness of her tongue.

You did it! said Star. *You brought her back!*

Mika stared into her companion's eyes and felt Star's pride surge across the bond.

What do you mean? asked Mika.

Then she looked past Star and saw Zabeh – eyes open, awake, alive.

CHAPTER 3

Mika wrapped her arms around Zabeh and held her tightly.

"I'm so sorry," she said. "I should have sensed that demon. I should have banished it..." She cried into Zabeh's collar.

Zabeh hugged her back weakly. "It's all right," she murmured. "You brought me back."

Mika pulled away and stared at her friend. Only now did the importance of what she'd done become clear. She had *reversed* the ghost-sleep. She had broken through the Narlaw's evil.

She could feel Star sending her encouragement through their bond, to counter the enormity of what she had just done. Mika reached out and found the soft fur of her companion's back.

Around the room Guran and his warriors looked on with an uneasy quiet.

Can you do it again? asked Star. *Can you wake Astor and the others?*

I don't know, said Mika. She shivered, remembering the horrifying tangle of Narlaw threads that had almost trapped her in the ghost-sleep with Zabeh. She had been lucky, and a part of her wanted to just forget the whole experience and enjoy the fact that Zabeh was back with her. But Star was right. Astor and the others were still deep in the ghost-sleep. She had to try again.

Suri, Astor's goat companion, paced between the beds of the sleepers, her hooves tapping against the stone in an anxious, irregular rhythm. A single storm lamp hung from a hook on the stone ceiling, casting a ring of golden light. Mika stood over Astor with Star by her side. Her body tingled with a mixture of excitement and fear. What if she couldn't free Astor from the ghost-sleep? What if she did it wrong and became trapped in the darkness with her mentor?

Do you need more rest? asked Star. *Maybe you should wait a while before you try this again?*

Mika shook her head. *I'm fine,* she said. *I can handle it.*

But she didn't know for sure. She still felt weak after waking Zabeh. The relief at reviving her friend had been glorious, but it was also strange and terrifying to know she was capable of such powerful channelling, as if right up until that moment, she'd been unaware of who she really was.

And now she had to do it all over again.

Zabeh had suggested they set out for Meridar right away, but Mika disagreed. What use was sharing this discovery if she couldn't repeat it?

No. She needed to be thorough and learn the method first. This was her way, and, as Star often reminded her, she could be as stubborn as a boulder in a blizzard.

Mika stared into Astor's sleeping face and then took in her thick woollen coat. It was colourfully embroidered like Mika's, but where Mika's coat had just one wind icon stitched to its cuff, Astor's was adorned with all four. She was a skilled channeller, able to draw great power from the chaotic, swirling winds.

Star leaped gently on to the foot of Astor's bed and peered up at Mika. *So where do we begin?* she asked.

Mika pushed her uncertainties aside and thought back to what she had done with Zabeh. *The sleep is maintained through some kind of binding,* she said. *It seemed like nothing but darkness at first, but when I reached deeper toward Zabeh I found the darkness was actually made up of lots of individual threads.*

And you broke through? asked Star.

The threads were tough, said Mika. *Sticky like a spider's web and woven tightly together. The sickness came on quickly, too. I dropped into the earth trance, but with Zabeh, I think it was my anger and guilt that carried me through.*

Star pressed her thick fur against Mika's hands and nuzzled her. *Then you have to get furious again,* she said.

Mika ran her hand down Star's back and over the flick of her tail. She wanted to be furious, but all she felt was fear.

She closed her eyes, placed her hands flat on the edge of the bed and reached into the vast dark of the ghost-sleep. Suri grunted in agitation behind her and Mika steadied herself against the dizzying touch of the demon's binding.

Star whispered a wordless reassurance across the bond and Mika focused, pushing down toward that faintest of glimmers – Astor's living presence. She had reached for Astor like this every day since her mentor had been lost to the ghost-sleep. Now it was time to go further. But the moment Mika pushed at the binding, the sickness overwhelmed her and she stepped back from the bed.

What is it? Star asked.

Mika shook her head. *The binding feels stronger than it did on Zabeh.*

You're still weak from the last time, said Star.

This was true, and the power of Mika's emotions had shielded her against the worst of the demon

41

sickness before. So what should she do now that she was approaching with a clear mind? Zabeh's fall had been so sudden and upsetting – and Mika had blamed herself for not sensing the demon in time. To recreate such a potent blend of emotions didn't seem possible.

If only we could carry her to a wind shrine, Mika said. *I could channel their strength.*

You've done it once without the winds, said Star. *You can do it again. I know you can.*

Mika placed one hand on Astor's forehead and one on her shoulder. Then she readied herself for the earth trance. Mika tried to pretend that she was back in the rooms she shared with Astor, embarking on another lesson under her mentor's watchful eye. She felt calmness flow into her and the trance engulfed her.

Battling the urge to turn back, Mika pushed and pushed, carrying herself into the smothering void of the ghost-sleep.

She felt the threads of the demon's binding and set about her task. The fury she had felt that morning was rekindled. How dare the Narlaw take her mentor from her? How dare they use these people for their own evil ends?

The heat of Mika's anger surged, dissolving the first clutch of threads as if they were nothing but frost to a flame. Mika struck again and again with her mind, snapping and unravelling, feeling the warmth of Astor's being grow ever so slowly closer.

As she worked, the threads became denser and more difficult to break. Mika found herself suddenly unmoving. She could push no further and, with a sinking feeling, she realized she had no sense of how to find her way out of the trance. Then fear took hold of her completely. What if she was trapped in here? Lost like Astor?

That panic was the final edge she needed. She let out a cry of fear, which gave her a sudden surge of energy, propelling her deeper into the dark tangle of the demon's binding.

Astor was close now. Her presence shone like a full moon behind the clouds. With a ferocious effort, Mika tore through the last of the bindings.

Astor broke free, engulfing Mika with feelings of shock and relief. Her presence grew until it filled the room.

Mika drew back, her eyes snapping open. She would have fallen again if Suri hadn't been there to steady her with a firm nudge of her horns. Mika lowered herself to the floor, unable to speak, and Star jumped down to be beside her, her tail swishing nervously.

Suri stamped her hooves and her joyful braying echoed loudly around the chamber.

Mika sat on the cold stone floor and let Star nuzzle into her. Her pride was like a warm glow inside her.

Astor perched on the edge of the bed, eating a rice cake Mika had brought her and scratching Suri's chin. The storm lamp flickered gently where it hung on the roof beam. Mika noted that Astor seemed frail. She had returned to them, but the ghost-sleep had taken its toll.

"We should climb to the wind shrine on Bone Hill," Astor said. "I can replenish my strength there."

Mika took a deep breath before answering. She doubted Astor could make it to the top of Bone Hill right now, but she couldn't bring herself to tell her mentor that. And anyway, there was worse news she had to break. "We can't get to the shrine," she said. "The whole city has fallen to the Narlaw."

"In seven days the city has fallen?" Astor frowned with disbelief and Mika detected a familiar edge of disappointment in her mentor's voice. "There are no militia left?"

"Only the ones in this basement," said Mika.

Astor stared around at the three sleeping warriors on their bunks. "Then we must revive as many as we can." She gave Mika a serious look, which seemed to be part interrogation and part pride. "It's a powerful thing you've discovered. Can you show me how it's done?"

For the remainder of that day Mika and Astor studied Mika's new technique. Mika delved for the hidden minds of the three ghost-sleeping soldiers and Astor watched over her, too fragile to risk attacking the demon bindings herself. One by one, Mika raised the warriors back into the waking world.

Each time it happened slightly differently, but by the end, Mika was certain it would work for anyone.

The warriors next door noisily welcomed their fallen comrades and Mika sat with Astor, drained of energy, but thrilled with their progress. They were all but alone now; Star was in the adjoining room, eating, and Suri had fallen asleep on the flagstones at Astor's feet.

"You've done well to survive here so long," Astor said. "It can't have been easy." Mika blushed at the praise. Astor was usually such a strict, demanding teacher. "But you must do more now," Astor told her. "You must carry this wisdom of yours to the capital."

"Yes," said Mika, though the thought of trying to get beyond the city filled her with dread.

"Remember," Astor said. "There are still warriors left and we know this city better than any demon. A young one like yourself will find a way."

"And you?" asked Mika. "Will you come, too?"

"I'll try." She smiled and let her eyes rest on the slumbering form of her companion.

Mika nodded, staring at the floor. She couldn't leave Astor behind. This was part of the reason she hadn't wanted to leave before now. She could never have left her mentor in the ghost-sleep, hidden in this cellar with demons stalking all around.

"One more observation," said Astor. "Something you may not have noticed while you were freeing me." She narrowed her eyes. "When you released me from the demon's binding, I felt another sensation – one unlike anything I've felt during the act of banishment." She stared into Mika's eyes, waiting for her understanding to blossom.

"But the demon was banished, no?" Mika said.

Astor tilted her head. "More than that," she said. "I felt a purity in the earth as I woke, as if the demon had been cast even further away – beyond the earth."

Mika listened, transfixed. No one knew where the Narlaw had come from, only that Amina had banished them beyond the mountains, creating an immense protective ward that separated Meridina from what was now the Darklands.

"Do you understand me, Mika? These demons coming through the mountain passes were banished once and are now returning. If my feeling is correct, we have found a way to send them from our world forever. I beg your pardon, Mika … *you* have found a way to do that."

For a moment Mika felt as if she were floating. Her blood thumped noisily in her veins.

Gone from our world forever.

Even Queen Amina had not done that.

Astor's eyes glittered in the light from the storm lamp. She reached out and touched Mika on the sleeve. "No longer a novice," she said.

Mika stared back, stunned into silence.

"Now, we should rest," said Astor. "My old bones are weary, and tomorrow we must carry your news to the world."

CHAPTER 4

The King's Keep bristled with guards. They stood sentry at every doorway and two of them flanked Dawn closely as she strode along the broad, torch-lined corridor that led toward the king's chambers. This was the very heart of the Palace of the Sun, which, in turn, stood at the the heart of Meridar, the capital city of the kingdom of Meridina. As the Palace Whisperer, Dawn had walked these corridors many times before, but she still felt her stomach flutter with nerves.

The guards' weapons clanked as they walked. They wore the red and gold of the Guards of the Sun, a reminder – as if Dawn needed one – of the Narlaw spy that had posed as a guard captain and abducted Princess Ona.

On Dawn's shoulder, Ebony twitched and eyed the guards warily. *Do you think the king will be pleased to see us?* she asked.

Dawn smiled weakly at her raven companion's grim attempt at humour. *The king's never been pleased to see us,* she said. *And especially not now.*

As soon as word of Princess Ona's disappearance reached King Eneron, Dawn had been summoned back to the Palace of the Sun. She had put it off as long as possible, working desperately to find some clue as to the princess's whereabouts, but eventually the Guards of the Sun had come for her. She had left Guard Captain Valderin in charge of the search. He was a good man and one of her few close allies in the palace.

Dawn felt a bitter mixture of guilt and frustration. She had come so close to unmasking the demon in their midst and still she had failed. If Ona was harmed it would be her fault. She imagined the terror the princess must be feeling, imprisoned in a trader's cart and stolen away from her home. As Dawn marched along with her escort of guards, she held on to that feeling of guilt. It would help her. It would be the fuel she needed to find the princess and bring her home.

They rounded a corner and Dawn was confronted by a line of heavily armed Guards of the Sun. Behind them stood the entrance to King Eneron's reception rooms, a pair of tall wooden doors, ornately carved and gleaming in the torchlight.

So this is the welcoming committee, said Ebony.

"The bird stays outside," one of the guards proclaimed, stepping forwards and dismissing the two who had escorted Dawn this far with a curt nod of his head. "The king will see you immediately," he said to Dawn.

You'd better go, Dawn whispered as the great doors creaked open. *See how the search is going. Hopefully I'll be with you soon.*

Ebony cawed loudly as she stretched her wings to fly and Dawn allowed herself a moment of satisfaction as the leader of the guards flinched away in surprise.

Don't forget to curtsey, said Ebony as she swept

along the corridor toward an open window, forcing those in her way to press themselves up against the walls.

I won't, whispered Dawn. She watched her companion vanish through the window and out into the open sky.

Dawn knew she would never have made it through the last few months without Ebony. Her companion helped her in so many ways, not least because of her sense of humour. Even Ebony's good-natured arrogance rubbed off on Dawn, bolstering her confidence at difficult times like this.

"Please…" said the guard leader.

Dawn felt a hand on her shoulder, gentle but insistent. She nodded and entered the chambers of the king.

In the anteroom she was met by Lady Tremaine, the Palace Warden, a woman who had rejoiced in making Dawn's life difficult since the day she arrived in the capital.

"Warden," said Dawn, nodding briskly in greeting.

The warden inclined her head and shot Dawn a tight, cruel smile. "King Eneron is distraught," she said. "You have a great deal to answer for, Whisperer."

"And I will," said Dawn.

The kingdom was at war and the princess had been abducted, yet Lady Tremaine still had time to feel smug at Dawn's expense. For the first time since meeting the warden, Dawn actually felt pity for her. But not enough pity to resist a jibe of her own.

"If only I'd realized sooner that the demon was hiding here in the King's Keep," she said. "Right under your nose."

The warden flushed at that. "Tell it to the king," she sneered, turning on her heel and marching toward one of two doors set in the far wall of the anteroom.

Dawn stood for a moment, before realizing she was supposed to follow the warden. The time had come.

In the king's council chamber sunlight streamed through the row of high windows and striped the room in gold and shadow. King Eneron stood silhouetted against the sun. Dawn squinted to make him out. His back was to the room and the long council table lay between them. As her eyes adjusted, Dawn saw that the king was dressed in battle armour.

"Your Grace," said the warden. "The Palace Whisperer is here."

Dawn tensed as the king turned to face her. She had never seen him like this before – upright and focused. He had always seemed like a broken man, forever grieving for his dead queen and uninterested in the running of the kingdom. Sunlight reflected off his polished armour and the sword hanging from his hip. Had Ona's disappearance finally woken him from his stupor?

"The Palace Whisperer," he said. His voice was flat and harsh.

Dawn rushed a curtsey. "Your Grace," she said, staring at her feet. Fear made her tremble and she felt angry that Lady Tremaine was there to witness her discomfort.

"You let them take my daughter," the king said,

striding forwards. "You let those demons take my precious Ona!" He slammed a gauntleted fist on the council table and the impact echoed around the room.

"I'm sorry," said Dawn, with her eyes still lowered. "But I'll find the princess. I have the whole palace guard out searching. We'll find her and bring her back." She looked up and met the king's furious gaze. There was a worrying edge of wildness in his eyes.

"We've suffered two Narlaw spies inside the palace in the last few weeks alone," he said. "Tell me – what use is a Whisperer if she cannot even keep demons out of the palace? Our water supply has been sabotaged. And who knows what else has happened without our knowing?"

Dawn wished she could leave – just walk out and get back to what really mattered – the search for Ona and the earthstone. Not only was Princess Ona in danger, but the consequences of losing the earthstone would be catastrophic.

Dawn cursed the fact that she had learned of the stone's importance too late. If only she had figured out sooner that Princess Ona's necklace held this relic from long ago, a stone that vastly increased the power of any Whisperer who wielded it. Queen Amina had worn the earthstone in the first Narlaw wars and, although she'd been unaware of its power, it had been decisive in her final victory. But the Narlaw had known of its importance all too well. A Narlaw spy had ransacked the princess's rooms and kidnapped Ona, who had been wearing the earthstone, before Dawn had had a chance to locate the stone herself.

The earthstone was Dawn's only chance of saving the kingdom from the Narlaw. And now, along with the king's only child, it was gone. If she didn't manage to get them back from the Narlaw's control, the whole kingdom would be overrun and nothing the king was saying would matter at all. But she had to show the proper respect.

"Your Grace," she said meekly. "I have done my best in a difficult time. No demons have walked in Meridina for a hundred years. They returned without warning—"

"Enough!" barked the king. "I didn't call you here

for excuses. You've let me down. I expected better from you, Esther, but you have let me down badly."

Dawn's mouth fell open but she couldn't find the words. She glanced across at Lady Tremaine, the warden, who glared back, but even she couldn't keep the concern from showing in her face.

He had called her Esther. Esther, who had been Dawn's mentor. Esther, who had died almost a year ago.

"After all the years you've served me," Eneron went on. He shook his head and Dawn finally recognized the emptiness in his gaze, a glistening that suggested tears. The more she looked, the more Eneron seemed like a child dressed up as a king. "It pains me," he said. "It really does. But unless you find my daughter, you are hereby exiled from Meridar. If you return without her, you will be put in chains and the darkest dungeon cell will be yours for the rest of your days. Do you understand, Esther?"

Dawn turned to the warden again and received nothing but a stony stare. "I'm not Esther," she said. "I'm Dawn."

"I asked you if you understood!" roared the king.

The warden stepped in. "She understands, Your Grace."

"Good." He turned his back on the two of them and paced over to the window. "Have her escorted to the south gate. Give her a horse and tell the guards that if she's seen in the city after sundown she'll be arrested."

"As you wish, Your Grace," said the warden. She bowed and gestured for Dawn to follow her.

As soon as they were outside the king's chamber Dawn turned on Lady Tremaine. "Did you hear what he said? He thinks I'm Esther. And you just stood there, going along with it all as if there's nothing wrong."

The warden frowned. "He may be a little confused," she said, "but the king's wishes make perfect sense. The fact is, you've failed Meridina too many times already. If you find the princess then all may be forgiven, but don't even think about coming back to Meridar without her."

Dawn glowered at the warden as two Guards of

the Sun approached. One of them took Dawn by the arm, but Dawn shrugged the hand away angrily.

"I can make my own way out," she said.

In the south of the city, birds wheeled above the crowded streets. Dawn watched as sparrows, finches, pigeons and starlings flocked together in perfect unison. It was a rare and beautiful sight and, for a moment, it distracted her from the urgency of the task at hand.

She had to bring Princess Ona back safely. Time was already running out and the king's mad decree had only added to her problems – now she had until sundown to leave the city, regardless of whether or not she had a lead on where Ona had been taken.

Dawn looked around her. Meridar was in turmoil – a capital city stretched to its limits by the chaos of approaching war.

High above the rooftops Dawn spotted Ebony, who was leading the flocks in their search for the Narlaw that had taken Princess Ona.

And the earthstone, Dawn thought. *The demon has taken the earthstone, too.* Dawn wanted to speak to Ebony, to share with her what had happened in the king's chambers. But there was no time.

Nearby on the busy street, a pair of palace guards were stopping as many people as they could to ask about the grocer's cart Princess Ona had been stolen away in. Guards had been sent all across the city to canvass for information. Hours had already passed since Ona went missing and every further minute that went by made finding her less likely.

Here, in the south of Meridar, the crowds were dense and people seemed anxious to keep moving. They were refugees from the surrounding countryside and most seemed reluctant to answer the guards' questions. Dawn didn't blame them – she wouldn't have noticed a particular grocer's cart if she'd just been forced from her home by an army of demons.

Much of the countryside had been ravaged by the Narlaw. Refugees from the farms, villages and towns were flooding toward the capital, seeking shelter behind the city walls. Dawn was glad of it, because Meridar was the only place in the kingdom with enough soldiers to put up a fight against the Narlaw.

Unfortunately, all of this panic made the hunt for the princess much more difficult. Even the birds seemed confused by the vast throngs of people below. Birds, like all animals, were sensitive to the presence of demons. With skill and luck, a flock of birds could even sense where a demon had been, tracing the particular taint the demon had left on the world as it passed. So far, Ebony and the city birds had tracked the Narlaw to an area around two gates in the south-west of the city wall. Despite this, there had been no definite sightings so far.

Dawn approached the pair of guards who were questioning the crowds for information. "Anything?" she asked.

She got a shake of the head from one guard. The other was still speaking to a frightened-looking man with a huge bundle at his feet. These were probably all the belongings the man could carry, the rest abandoned in his home.

Carts rumbled by slowly, negotiating their way through the bustling mass of refugees. The citizens of Meridar watched from their windows and shop fronts as the new arrivals flooded in. A siege seemed inevitable now. There were so many Narlaw out there, and so few soldiers and Whisperers to fight them.

Dawn peered back into the sky as a flock of sparrows swooped and fluttered loudly over the nearby rooftops.

Ebony, she called. *What can you see?*

It took a moment before her companion replied. *No sign of the Narlaw,* she said. *But you have a message from Captain Valderin. Look west.*

Dawn did so, craning to see down a shadowy side street. Captain Valderin, the head of the Palace Guard, had taken his own group of guards to the west. Ebony must have spotted one of his messengers.

Dawn saw a female guard dodging through the crowded alley and held up a hand to greet her.

"News from Captain Valderin," the guard said with a small bow. "The cart was sighted near the stonecutters' gate less than an hour ago. It left the city on the four-counties road. The captain sent four of his fastest riders in pursuit and he's waiting at the gate for you now."

"We're sure it was the right cart?" Dawn asked, trying to suppress her excitement.

The woman nodded. "A local trader tried to stop the cart and buy some fruit. He was almost knocked over as it passed. His description of the cart matches perfectly."

"Sounds like our demon," said Dawn. Finally, this was what she needed! But she was an hour behind already. A cart could go a long way in that time, even on the busy roads. "Take me to Valderin."

The woman nodded and Dawn called for the other two guards to follow her.

The stonecutters' gate rumbled with the sound of angry voices. Everyone entering the city was being stopped by the palace guard. There was a huge trail of people threading away beyond the city wall – impatient, scared people who had travelled a long way to get there. But Dawn knew the road block was necessary. Some of these refugees must have seen the Narlaw's cart as it left the city along the four-counties road, heading south-west.

Dawn crossed the broad square that led to the gate itself. This was a busy trading district and guards could be seen at every door, questioning and re-questioning the owners and customers. Dawn spotted Captain Valderin near the gate. Through the tall arch she could see a jam of carts and foot travellers.

"Dawn," said Valderin as she approached. "We should set off right away."

"Do we have horses?" she asked.

Valderin nodded to one side where a group of guards stood ready with horses that looked fresh from the palace stables. "It seems like the demon's avoiding the main south road," he said. "The Narlaw army's in that direction – near Altenheim – but the south road's also where we've stationed most of our lookouts."

Dawn nodded. "These refugees are going to make it hard to get anywhere with a cart. We may stand a chance of catching up if we move quickly." She glanced at another thunderous passing of birds overhead. Among them was Ebony's familiar presence.

We're leaving, Dawn whispered. *Can you lead the birds out of town?*

Ebony flapped down with a long, throaty caw and gripped Dawn's shoulder hard. *I'll try,* she said. *But they won't be happy about it. These birds don't like the wilds much. Too many predators out there.*

You can do it, said Dawn. *You have to. We can't lose Ona and the earthstone like this. If we don't bring them back, it will all be over. Please…*

Panic rose up inside her and she felt her breathing quicken. It would all be over. Everything.

Ebony shifted position on Dawn's shoulder, her claws pinching through Dawn's coat.

We'll find them, said Ebony. *I promise we'll find them. And I'll do my best to convince the birds —*

but even a superior raven like me can't herd sparrows and pigeons very far across the wilderness.

Dawn smiled. Her anxiety subsided just a little. *Who ever said you were superior?*

It's a fact, said Ebony. *No one needs to say it.* She flapped her huge black wings and Dawn flinched away, still smiling.

Just do your best, said Dawn, hoping desperately that their best would be good enough.

Ebony cawed and lifted herself into the air with long, powerful wing strokes.

Dawn glanced around at the chaos. There was no doubt that war was coming to Meridar. She only wished that they'd been ready – that they'd had more time to prepare for the invasion. But Dawn would defend Meridina as best she could – starting with finding Princess Ona and bringing her back with the earthstone.

She had to.

"Ready?" Valderin called. He was mounted on his horse, the dark bay mare he had ridden into battle at Altenheim.

Dawn nodded and took the reins of another horse as they were passed to her: a beautiful, copper-coloured mare with a mane and tail that shone almost silver in the sunlight. She swung up into the saddle and felt the animal's presence beneath her – brave and dependable. She had barely ridden since leaving the Southlands, and as they set off on the trail of the Narlaw, Dawn felt the freedom of travel mix strangely with the terrible uncertainty of what lay ahead.

CHAPTER 5

The cart bumped and rattled violently. Princess Ona sat hunched in the back, bracing herself against the rough wooden slats to either side of her. Her arms ached and her back was sore. She wanted to cry out, but remembered what the demon had told her as it had thrown her into the cart: *If you scream, I'll kill you.*

Ona shivered at the memory of that voice. One second it had sounded like Captain Niels, the leader of her father's personal guard; the next, the demon had dropped its act and become the heartless creature it truly was. And that creature was behind her now, driving this stinking, rickety cart away from Meridar ... taking her toward who knew what.

As the cart hit a solid bump in the road,

Ona flinched and prepared herself to try another escape. She slid toward the back of the cart and held tight to the walls. Then, in time with the next loud thud of the cartwheels she kicked out at the door.

She kicked, again and again, timing her strikes so they couldn't be heard. But it was no use. It turned out that this was no normal grocer's cart. The door had clanked ominously when the demon had closed her in, suggesting that it had been cleverly reinforced. Her abduction had been well planned – she was certain of that. And the shape-shifting spy up front wasn't about to let her escape by kicking the door down.

Ona sank back on to the floor. Her shoes were scuffed horribly, with the silver thread hanging loose in several places. Her tights were ripped, too, snagged on the splintery wooden floor. She shook her head, realizing how ridiculous it was to be worried about the state of her clothes at a time like this. But the whole situation was so unexpected and so awful that she just didn't know what to think.

All she could do was trust in Dawn and Captain

Valderin to come after her. By now, they must know she was missing, she thought. And Dawn was a Whisperer – they could do such amazing things, so surely she could find her out here on the back roads…

The earthstone bounced on its chain around Ona's neck, along with the other stones of her favourite necklace. Now she knew what the demons had been after, she felt foolish. All the trouble they had taken to catch the Narlaw spies in the palace and this stone had been hanging from her neck all along. If she'd known she would have handed it over to Dawn right away.

At least she knew one thing about the earthstone – the demon couldn't touch it. Otherwise the Narlaw would have just torn the necklace from her throat. But it had flinched away when it came close to her. She could tell how much it hurt the creature to pick her up and throw her into the cart.

The trouble was that if the earthstone was here with her, it left the rest of Meridina unprotected. Queen Amina had used the earthstone to defeat the

Narlaw and now Dawn needed it.

Ona peered down at the cloud-grey jewel. Would Dawn and the other Whisperers be able to fight the Narlaw without it? While she was stuck in this cart, rattling further and further from home, the kingdom was being destroyed around her. She had to escape.

Ona listened to the world beyond the cart as she travelled.

To begin with there were many sounds – voices, carts creaking and the clop of horses' hooves. She knew the other people on the road were heading to Meridar for safety. If they had only known that their princess was passing right by them! More than once, Ona thought about calling out. If all the people around the cart teamed together, perhaps they could overpower the demon? But she knew it was likely these people would be hurt, and her, too. So she stayed silent, she listened and she held on to the earthstone at her chest.

A long time passed before the roads around them became quiet. Ona could just make out the swish of trees and the babble of a nearby river. She pressed her face against the slats of the cart wall and peered through one of the tiny gaps. It was pointless. She could see virtually nothing, and anyway, she wouldn't recognize where they were. Thanks to her father's obsession with safety, Ona had never set foot beyond the palace walls. She had always dreamed of exploring the rolling countryside beyond the city. From her balcony high up in the palace, the hills and forests had looked beautiful and inviting – so different to her own rigid world of stone towers and formal gardens. Eventually Ona had given up asking the king for permission to venture out.

Clattering along in the back of the grocer's cart, Ona felt sad and angry that her first trip outside had come about through such terrible circumstances.

Suddenly the cart turned off the road and rolled slowly on to some kind of steep path. Ona scrambled to stay upright as the floor sloped beneath her. She slid and felt her dress catch on a splinter of wood. Then the cart creaked to a standstill and all she could hear were the trees and the river.

She risked a look through the gap between the slats and pulled back as a tall shadow swept across her vision. Her heart beat ferociously. Was it coming for her? She held the earthstone out in front of her and squatted, ready to act when the doors opened. There wasn't really enough room to spring out at the demon, but she could try.

The doors stayed firmly shut.

Ona waited, breathing deeply in an attempt to calm her nerves.

A rhythmic scraping noise started up, then something brushing against the outside of the cart. Ona smelled paint and realized what the demon was doing: it was repainting the cart – disguising it, so that anyone who had seen them leave Meridar would no longer recognize it.

How would anyone find her now? She began to panic and would have screamed if she thought there was anyone nearby, but what would be the use?

She had to figure out where she was. She had to get someone's attention.

And then she knew what she had to do.

Ona sat back down, still clutching the earthstone, but forcing calm into her mind. Calm and focus. She had to think. She had to do this right.

Soon, the demon climbed back into the cab and pointed the cart horse back toward the road. When Ona felt them rise back out of the woods she pressed her eye to the gap between the slats of the cart and waited for a sign of habitation.

Only when she saw a well, then a short row of cottages, did she begin.

She untied the blue silk sash of her dress from around her waist. It had been a birthday gift from her father, made especially for her, and her first initial was stitched on it beneath the royal insignia. It smelled sweetly of her favourite perfume.

Ona plucked a hairpin from its place and with the pin she pushed her sash through one of the narrow gaps between the slats. It seemed to take forever, and she glanced anxiously toward the cab, thinking her abductor would spot what she was doing any second.

But finally the last corner of the sash slid through

the gap and dropped away from her.

Ona peered out and saw a streak of beautiful sky-blue silk in the centre of the muddy track. Her heart thumped. She saw a squat barn and another cottage set back from the road and hoped they were not empty – that there was someone on this lonely road who would receive her silent cry for help.

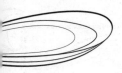

CHAPTER 6

Mika slept badly on her eighth and final night in hiding. She lay awake with anxious thoughts circling her mind and, when she finally drifted into sleep, her dreams were awash with fear and darkness.

Star woke her in the morning. It was a favourite habit of Star's, pressing her wet nose against Mika's cheek until Mika opened her eyes. Usually it was done in the name of mischief or boredom, but today Mika woke to find she had overslept. The lanterns were already alight and Guran's militia moved purposefully about the basement. Their leather armour creaked and the scrape of blades being sharpened cut through the air like jags of lightning.

How could you sleep through this? asked Star. She paced up and down beside Mika's bed.

I'm not sure you could call it sleeping, said Mika. *I'm more tired than I was before.*

She rose with a nervous feeling in her stomach. She hadn't travelled beyond the highlands before, nor was she a fighter like Zabeh or Guran.

I should pack, she said, glancing down at her rumpled bedroll and few possessions.

Mika felt suddenly ashamed at her days of inaction. Part of the reason she'd stayed was Astor – she just hadn't been able to bring herself to abandon her mentor. But she had also fooled herself into thinking that hiding was the only option. She had let her fear get the better of her.

Not any more, though. It was time to answer the call to Meridar.

She rolled her bedding tight enough to carry and stuffed her few spare clothes into the pack she had scavenged several days ago. On top of her clothes she laid the remains of a jasmine candle and the two small bundles of food she had been rationed – rice cakes, and pickled radish and ginger, all wrapped together in cloth. She had nothing from her home and she knew she couldn't go back. The rooms she shared with Astor were too close to the centre of Rakeen, where most of the Narlaw had gathered.

Next, Mika donned her thick, hooded coat. She hefted her pack and ducked her head through the single strap so that it lay diagonally across her chest. She was ready to go.

Zabeh approached from across the room. She nodded to Mika and pulled a long, slim object from her pocket. "Here," she said. "You'll need it."

Mika looked at the knife and shook her head. "I don't carry weapons. You know that."

Zabeh's smile was good-natured, but edged with impatience. This was not the first time the conversation had taken place between them. Mika understood her friend's concern, but she had sworn never to commit violence.

"Come on," said Zabeh. "Just for once, be ready to defend yourself. Who knows what trouble we might find on the road?"

Mika slipped her hands into her pockets in a final gesture of refusal. She felt a flicker of anger.

Her friend obviously still thought she couldn't look after herself.

"We have different ways of protecting ourselves," said Mika. "A knife would be no use to me."

Zabeh nodded and Mika watched her reluctantly pocket the weapon. It was clear that Zabeh still wasn't confident in Mika's banishing abilities. Mika thought about all the times Zabeh had stood up for her and protected her when they were younger. And she thought about how she had failed to protect Zabeh when the Narlaw had attacked her in the merchant's garden. Perhaps Zabeh was right. Perhaps she couldn't be trusted to look after herself, let alone her friends.

Astor stepped into the room with Suri by her side and all eyes turned toward the elderly Whisperer and her companion. Mika was glad of the distraction.

Guran gave a respectful nod. "Are you ready?" he asked.

"Yes," Astor said, though she leaned on Suri's back for support. "May the four winds carry you safely."

"Thank you. Travel well, and give our regards to Meridar and the king."

The militia warriors filed upstairs, their weapons sheathed and their movements near-silent. At Guran's suggestion, they were to draw the Narlaw away, down into the centre of Rakeen and then east so that Mika, Astor and Zabeh could slip away into the western hills. Guran had spoken of escaping with his warriors into the eastern mountains then down on to the plains of central Meridina, but they knew this was almost impossible. There were simply too many Narlaw in the city.

Mika watched the last of the warriors file out of the cellar. She had to succeed in her mission so that the warriors' incredible bravery wasn't wasted.

"Now it's our turn," said Astor. "I fear I may be too slow to keep pace. Promise me – Mika, Zabeh – if we fall into danger, leave me. You must reach the palace. The kingdom depends on it."

"It won't come to that," said Mika as she followed Astor and Suri up the short stone staircase.

Star darted past them all to the top. Mika envied

her companion's enthusiasm. It was as if this were simply the beginning of a huge adventure, another chance to explore the city.

Be careful, Mika whispered to her. *Don't go too far ahead.*

I'm not going to leave you behind, said Star.

That's not what I'm worried about. You know how many demons are out there. Please, just stay close.

Star turned to wait for her. *I've been down every back street in Rakeen,* she said. *Every garden path and passageway. I'll get us out of the city safely, I promise.*

Mika smiled, trying to ignore her own anxiety. *I know you will,* she said.

Star flicked her tail playfully against Mika's leg, then she slipped through the cellar door in a flash of white.

Mika cast her senses through the house above, feeling for the slightest hint of danger. She was precise, focused and determined. Since her breaking of the ghost-sleep it was as if her senses had sharpened. This time, Mika promised herself, she would not fail her friends.

The way above was clear and Mika signalled them out into the bright, chill morning. Wind swept down off the mountains, and the trees and plants of the ravaged garden swayed and bent around them.

"We should stay close together," she said, turning to catch Zabeh's eye.

Zabeh nodded, scanning the edges of the garden with a grim expression.

Then Star darted out across the garden and they began their escape from Rakeen.

The route was winding and complicated. Star had chosen it for stealth, but also ease of movement – no climbing or crawling that might make life difficult for Astor or Suri. For this reason, their progress was slow.

Almost as soon as they left the garden they were forced to stop. Mika sensed something wrong and held her hand up in a fist. She crouched on the cobbled back street, second in line behind Star, with Zabeh guarding the rear.

Mika extended her senses cautiously. In a house

at the end of the alley were a pair of demons. She could feel them, unmoving, inside the modest, wood-framed dwelling. Their presence was like a foul taste in her mouth and their terrible stillness made her tremble.

Should we change course? asked Star.

Mika crouched for a moment longer, observing the demons, forcing herself to ignore the growing discomfort in her belly.

No, she said at last. *I've seen this before. We can pass by.*

Whatever the Narlaw's equivalent of sleep was, this was it. Mika looked up and met Star's gaze, nodding for her to continue.

Star rose slowly from her own defensive crouch, uncertain. But Mika knew she was right. They moved off again, staying close to the wall at the far edge of the alley. Mika probed her surroundings constantly, watching Star dart and creep ahead of her and keeping track of Astor's laboured breathing and the clack of Suri's hooves behind.

For some time they continued in this way,

moving gradually from the affluent silk district into the hilly, cramped suburbs of the city's western fringe. This was where the majority of Rakeen's people had lived, in terraces of wooden houses, most without any kind of yard or garden. Though it was easier for them to stay hidden in these narrow, shadowed streets, there were also many more places for a demon to hide.

Mika scanned the houses as they passed, checking for hidden demons. They were all empty – of demons, but of people, too. She wondered where all the people were, thinking perhaps that the Narlaw had placed them in the ghost-sleep and carried them off to some holding area, to be stacked like logs for the winter.

Wherever they were, she knew the only way these people might ever return to their homes was if the war against the Narlaw was won. She felt the pressure of the knowledge she carried all over again, along with a spark of pride – but now was not the time for self-congratulation. Not until the last Narlaw was gone from the earth.

Star led them into a tiny courtyard that was shared by five or six small houses. There was a persimmon tree at the centre, its roots bulging through the cobbles and its leafless branches drooping under the weight of the faded orange fruit.

Astor reached out and plucked one, turning it over in her hand.

"Still good," she said with a rare smile. She bit down on the fruit and winced at its sharpness.

Suri craned her neck to eat one straight off the branch.

As Mika turned to Astor, about to suggest they keep moving, a flash high up at the edge of her vision stopped her short.

A flaming arrow arced through the clear blue sky.

Zabeh caught sight of it, too. "The signal," she said. "The others have reached the centre."

Mika pictured Guran charging though the streets, his militia warriors behind him, Narlaw rushing out of the buildings. To be smothered in the ghost-sleep or be killed? It seemed as if only those two options could possibly await the warriors.

Mika whispered an entreaty to the earth, a prayer for the soldiers' safety, but as she did so, her senses reeled. "Hide!" she hissed. "In here!"

She darted through a low doorway into a house she could feel was empty. The others followed and Mika reached out, controlling her fear, as the street outside became alive with Narlaw.

Doors banged and boots pounded on the cobbles in strange, inhuman rhythms. Through a murky window, Mika glimpsed the blur of a man. She felt the demon's presence and swallowed hard.

"Get down!" hissed Zabeh.

Mika dropped to the bare wooden floor with the others. She reached out for Star, who pressed close to her side.

The battle had commenced. The demons were being drawn to the centre. How had they responded so quickly?

Even now, Mika wondered at the workings of the Narlaw mind. Did they communicate in whispers like she and Star? Or was it something else, some other connection that could cross great distances?

In seconds the stampede was over. Mika felt the air around her settle, as if the neighbourhood itself had breathed a sigh of relief.

"We should go," she said. "Now."

No one argued.

Star scampered back into the courtyard and they hurried on behind, even Astor managing to run. They made their winding way among the homes and stables and workshops, Mika sweeping her surroundings, not leaving anything to chance.

The city wall is close, said Star. *Stay with me.* She dodged around an upturned cart into a deeply shadowed alley and Mika followed her in. Houses rose high on either side and there was a smell of dung and old animal odours. Suri's hooves echoed off the walls behind her.

Star swerved again, flowing smoothly round a sharp corner. A broad avenue appeared at the end of the alley. Sunlight glowed on the flagstones and glittered in the channel of water at the avenue's edge – one of the many diverted streams that supplied the city. Star paused before the junction, ears standing tall as she peered out of the alley.

Mika joined her, squinting across the avenue. Above one final line of houses, stood the city wall.

There, said Star.

But Mika did not need to be told. She recognized the tall, smart house diagonally across from them, with its curved terracotta roof. She had visited its grounds many times before with Star and Zabeh. It was the second home of a rich city official, an official corrupt enough to have a secret doorway built into the city wall that bounded the rear garden of his house. He used it for smuggling goods in and out of Rakeen and avoiding tax inspections at the guarded public gates. Star had discovered the doorway years ago on one of her sneaky explorations of the city and it had become a childhood escape route for the three of them, their way out to a world of freedom and make-believe in the wilds beyond.

I can smell the grass on the hillside, said Star. *The junipers and the gojan berries.*

Mika ran her hand down Star's back. Star snorted excitedly, flicking her bushy fox tail and looking up and down the long, curving avenue, impatient to cross.

"The secret gate," said Zabeh, as she arrived at the back of the group.

Mika nodded. "We'll pass through the grounds of that town house," she said to Astor, indicating which one. "There's a smuggling gate that will take us into the western hills."

Astor gave her a disapproving frown. But rather than question Mika on how she knew about the gate, she nodded, then peered over the rooftops at the curving, tree-specked country beyond. "The Bone Hill shrine is close," she said, breathing raggedly between words, still recovering from the run. "It's a shame we must go right away. It would do me good to stop there for a while."

"We'll soon be away from the city," said Mika gently. "There'll be other shrines on the way." She knew Astor had suffered badly from the ghost-sleep. Her mentor was no longer young and these dark times were taking a heavy toll.

"Of course," said Astor, regaining her composure.

"Let's go on."

Star needed no more encouragement. She edged out on to the shaded avenue.

Mika pushed her senses further, to take in the large open space and the rows of grand houses on the far side. She felt the water trickling through the gutter, the spruce trees swaying in the grounds of the houses, and dust that rose and looped on the wind.

Is it safe? asked Star. She edged out into the avenue impatiently.

Wait! said Mika. *Star!*

Darkness came at Mika like a racing thundercloud. She heard the clatter of cartwheels from the north, charging downhill along the avenue.

Narlaw.

Mika couldn't tell how many, only that it was the most powerful demon presence she had ever felt. She ducked into the shadows.

Hide! she hissed. With horror, she realized that Star had trotted out into the centre of the avenue. When the demons arrived, they would see Star, a small but bright white arctic fox, standing there in full view.

Run! urged Mika.

Star darted across the avenue, her paws pattering and her tail flashing behind her as she ran, vanishing into the shadow of an archway.

Mika exhaled with relief and a strange softness settled over her senses. Astor had laid a stealth wish over them – a protective Whisperer ward to make them temporarily invisible.

Moments later an open-topped wagon swept into view. It was drawn by a speckled white horse, its unearthly grey eyes shining as it dragged a four-wheeled cart laden with bodies.

Mika hoped those people were sleeping and not worse, but she feared to reach out with her senses to check – riding the cart, standing tall and without reins, was a Narlaw. Its presence was so strong that Mika clutched at her throat to keep from being sick. She watched with terror as it thundered past. Though she knew she couldn't be seen or sensed through Astor's ward, she felt herself cowering further into the shade of the alley.

The demon had taken a woman's form, with black hair cut straight above the shoulders and a long, flowing coat the colour of steel. It raced away, carried by the pounding hooves of the horse-shaped demon at the head of the cart.

Mika breathed again, but as the cart disappeared into the distance she saw the demon turn its head. A chill swept through her. Could it have seen them? And then the cart was gone around the curve of the avenue.

Star, Mika whispered.

Her companion nosed out of the shadows on the far side of the avenue and Mika reached out with her senses to feel the reassuring warmth of their Whisperer bond. She turned to find Astor staring, glassy-eyed, into the street. Suri stood close to Astor, rigidly upright. Behind her Zabeh crouched, sword drawn and a questioning look on her face.

"A demon of such power," said Astor, "can only be one of the elder Narlaw." She shot Mika a grave look. "My stealth wish cannot hold for long.

We must leave this place."

Mika scanned the avenue and rose on shaky legs. "Let's go," she said.

They crossed the avenue at a flat run and passed into the ornamental garden of the corrupt city official. Mika's mind raced. An elder demon. She had heard of their existence but never seen or sensed one. She imagined what would have happened if it had seen them. How could such a thing be fought or banished? To go up against it would be like fighting a tornado with your bare hands. She feared more than ever for Guran and the militia.

Moments later Mika found herself at the wall. Star sat, peering up at the hidden door. It looked like every other section of the wall apart from a near-invisible frame of dark wood that traced the door's outline.

Mika and Zabeh reached out and each laid a hand on a specially chosen rock. They nodded and pressed hard in perfect unison.

Granite slid and scraped, a mechanism clicked within the wall and, with the slightest of creaks, the door unlocked.

Zabeh pressed her shoulder to the door and it slid forwards roughly on wooden runners, into the metre-thick defensive wall. The door swung as it reached the outside edge of the wall and daylight shone through.

Mika felt a flood of relief. They had made it out of the city. The first great challenge was over.

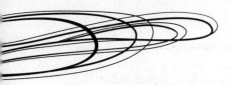

CHAPTER 7

Star was first to go through, scampering out as soon as Mika had scanned their surroundings for demons. Mika ducked through next and surveyed the small flat stretch of muddy ground and the hills and mountains that rose beyond.

They already had a route in mind – a way toward Meridar that would keep them as sheltered and out of sight as possible. But even at best, the country around Rakeen was exposed. There were no forests here, only scattered copses of trees hardy enough to survive the highland climate.

Zabeh swung the door shut heavily behind them and they set out west, following the gully of a small stream as it wound between the folds of the hills. The wind blew hard and Mika was glad of her gloves and the thick hood of her coat. Clouds sailed across the sky, threatening rain. She watched Star dart ahead, sniffing the earth, and Astor squint into the wind, testing its direction with the slightest tilting of her head.

Her mentor glanced often toward the white pinnacle of the wind shrine on Bone Hill – the curved pyramid of the shelter and the bundled cross of the tone-pipes on top. On any other day they would have detoured there to guide the winds through the tone-pipes and take nourishment from the earth's powerful breath. Mika strained to hear the tones, but they were too distant, the unchannelled wind too strong in her ears.

Slowly they climbed until they crested the first shallow hill. They could see the city spread out behind them and Mika fought back her sadness as she turned to look. It was so desolate and silent. She thought of Guran and his warriors. Were they alive or dead? No sounds of battle echoed on the winds. Perhaps they were in the ghost-sleep already.

"We'll return," said Zabeh, as if hearing her

thoughts, "and we'll free them all."

Mika wished she shared Zabeh's certainty. "We should have left sooner," she said, "but I was afraid to go."

Zabeh shrugged. "Maybe," she said, "but if we hadn't waited, you would never have discovered your gift."

What Zabeh said was true. There was no telling what each day would bring, what disaster might come or what new blessing might spring forth from its ashes.

Astor climbed slowly up to meet them with Suri by her side. Something in her features seemed wrong. She was trying to speak, out of breath from the climb.

Mika stepped toward her, but before she could ask, a troubling presence at the edge of her senses told her what Astor lacked the breath to say. Mika spun to look downhill. There, just a few hundred paces away, was a horse and its rider.

It was the elder demon.

Mika stared at the demon and the demon

watched her in return. Why wasn't it coming for them? Its stillness made it even more frightening. She turned to Astor.

"We have to go," the older Whisperer said, still gasping for breath. "There's only one place we can hope to stand against it."

Mika gazed up at the wind shrine on the summit of Bone Hill. She nodded.

"Can you run?" she asked.

Astor's face set like granite. "I can try."

"Zabeh!" Mika called. Her friend had strayed from her side, peering down the path at the demon. She swung round at Mika's cry. "We have to get to the shrine!" Zabeh nodded and fell in behind Astor, who was already hurrying along the footpath.

Mika jogged with Star beside her. The path dipped before climbing once again toward Bone Hill. It quickly grew steeper and Mika looked back to see the elder demon racing across the open ground, its demon-horse devouring the distance between them. Mika peered up at the increasingly rocky path. The shrine looked so far away.

Can we make it? asked Star.

Mika felt her fear like a cold needle. *I don't know,* she said. *Perhaps, but…*

She trailed off and Star remained silent. They both knew their chances were slim.

Mika started up the first truly steep section of the hill. Gravel slipped away beneath her hands and feet. Her boots thumped into the hard earth. The path was narrow, weaving between hummocks of stiff highland grass. Rain clouds gathered in the sky. She looked back and saw Astor struggling behind her, close by. At the rear came Zabeh, glancing back every second step. Mika swallowed her rising sense of panic. She couldn't let Zabeh be taken again.

She clambered over the flat slabs of rock placed at intervals along the path. The wind blasted from the north and the shrine grew closer, but not as quickly as the demon rider. Mika turned and saw that it had reached the foot of the trail. The horse scrambled up the first few paces, then its hooves began to slide. The demon leaped from its back, its face a hollow grey counterfeit of a woman's.

It looked up at Mika, and a sickening darkness rushed at her, forcing her to stop and retch violently.

Mika! Star cried.

I'm all right, she said, spluttering from the sickness.

She pulled her Whisperer senses in, closing off her mind as Astor had taught her. The sickness ebbed, but she saw the demon was climbing fast.

Mika was first to the top and she stood on the level ground reaching out a hand to help Astor as she struggled, gasping on to the windswept summit.

"We're almost there!" cried Mika, leading her mentor toward the juniper wood shelter of the wind shrine.

The tone-pipes on top of the shelter howled discordantly as the wind glanced off them. The hollowed wood rattled in its bindings.

Inside the shelter, the noise was amplified. Mika helped Astor into a kneeling position on the woven rug floor. She felt the elder demon draw near, the weight of its evil pressing in on her. Through the small, half-moon of the door she saw Star, Zabeh and Suri standing together.

Star! she called. *What are you doing?*

We can slow the demon down, said Star, *to give you and Astor time.*

But it's too powerful! cried Mika. *You have to take shelter. All of you!*

Star glared defiantly at Mika.

Mika had forgotten how fierce her companion could be. Star was a wild fox at heart. She would defend herself and her friends no matter what.

"Mika," whispered Astor.

Mika turned back to her mentor.

"Bring the south wind," said Astor. "As we practised. Please." Her voice came in gasps and she swayed on her knees as if she were about to collapse.

Mika closed her eyes. Then she heard a crack and glanced outside. Suri was butting one of the waymarker stones with her horns. She charged again and another crack echoed over the sound of the winds. The stone tumbled. Zabeh shouted something, lost in the wind, and Mika fought the urge to reach out to Star, to steady her and comfort her.

Instead she turned inwards, opened her mind and prepared to channel the winds. This was the only way she could protect Star and the others.

She felt Astor reaching up into the chaotic winds above, separating them and channelling the strong north wind toward the tone-pipes on top of the shrine. Once the tone-pipes were singing with the channelled wind, Mika and Astor could draw on that concentrated power. But they had never used a shrine for banishment before, only healing. Mika wondered if it was possible to channel enough power to fight the elder demon. She closed her eyes and reached up with her Whisperer sense.

Hers was the south wind, the only one she had ever mastered. She felt it swirling in the melee up above. She also felt the touch of the demon, but Astor's channelling gave her strength to withstand it.

Mika made her mind become like a gentle hand to guide the wind.

Astor had already channelled the north wind into the tone-pipes, creating a deep, resonant note that rumbled through the shrine's wooden walls. It was this resonance that would enhance the Whisperers' power. Mika struggled to do the same with the south wind and she had almost succeeded when a cry from outside dragged her concentration away.

The elder demon had reached the hilltop.

Zabeh lay on her back, several paces away. Suri charged the demon and was knocked aside as if she were a leaf on the breeze. Star stood growling, but was ignored.

The demon came for them, but Astor's channelling was strong. She sent the full force of the north wind at the advancing creature. The wind sang as it engulfed the demon, turning the creature's movements back on itself. The Narlaw's coat flapped wildly and its legs struggled at every step.

Mika knew she had to help. She glanced once more at Zabeh then closed her eyes.

It came more easily now. Flowing, obediently almost, the tones began to echo in the shelter – the special chord of the south sounding a perfect complement to the north wind.

Mika felt the demon stop.

The strain of the channelling drew sweat to her brow despite the freezing air, and she thought, in terror, that neither she nor Astor could possibly keep this up for much longer.

"Banish," Astor whispered feebly to Mika.

Mika fixed the southern wind in place and reached out. She pictured Zabeh lying there and met the demon with all the anger she felt. She attacked in the same way she had attacked the bonds of the ghost-sleep.

The demon flinched in surprise and it was all the chance Mika needed. She tore at the demon's presence. It was a vast, angry core of darkness. It struck back, but the channelled winds protected Mika. The earth was on her side.

She felt the demon coil and ready itself to strike. It slipped away from her, but she followed, pushing closer.

Fear spiked amid her anger.

Zabeh, she whispered to herself.

For a long heartbeat Mika felt so much energy in

her that it overwhelmed her. The earth's fury raged and then was gone, sucked away like a fire suddenly deprived of fuel.

Mika dropped to the floor of the shelter, stunned, but awake. She felt a hand on her arm.

Astor. "It's gone, Mika. It's gone…"

Mika blinked away the fiery after-image and peered out through the juniper-woven door. There stood Zabeh, breathing hard, her palms resting on her knees. She could feel Star's presence somewhere close, although she was out of sight. And Suri.

There was no demon. Only flecks of rain that fell and washed the ground where it had stood.

CHAPTER 8

Dawn rode her horse slowly through the dim morning light. After a full night of searching it took all her strength not to fall asleep in the saddle. Mud flicked up from the mare's huge hooves and Dawn peered off into the woodland at the side of the track. She heard a river in there somewhere, but felt no sign of Narlaw.

Since leaving Meridar, she and the palace guards had gradually spread out and split into smaller and smaller groups. With an hour's headstart, the demon could have been hiding anywhere. There were so many roads and paths that even the few birds who had followed Ebony out of the city couldn't hope to cover such a broad area.

Dawn wished she had Ebony by her side, but her

companion had her own search to conduct, roaming the skies with the city birds. Dawn could feel her presence if she reached out, but it was faint.

She knew the demon would be miles away by now – that the chances of them rescuing Princess Ona before she was handed over to the Narlaw army were incredibly slim. Dawn wished, for the thousandth time, that she had found the Narlaw spy before it had taken the princess – that she had realized the importance of the earthstone before it was too late. King Eneron's ultimatum echoed in her mind. She was in exile and nothing but the safe return of Princess Ona would change that. If only that were the worst of it, she thought. If she couldn't find the princess and the earthstone, if she failed again, there would be no palace to return to, no kingdom left to call home. But she refused to give up. No matter how far from Meridar Ona was carried, Dawn would follow. All the way to the heart of the demon army if she had to.

Dawn reached out further with her Whisperer sense. Although most of the people were gone from these parts, she could still feel the earth alive and well around her – the trees shaking in the breeze, the stream rushing and gurgling on its long course toward the Inland Sea. There was even a deer, silent and alert under cover of the trees, watching as the horse and rider passed by on the road.

Dawn wondered whether Valderin or the others had found anything. But Ebony would have told her if they had. She knew Ebony would be feeling as frustrated and ashamed as she was. They had failed badly. Dawn's thoughts turned to the matter of defending the city of Meridar. How could she banish so many Narlaw without the earthstone? Only a third of the kingdom's Whisperers had arrived at the palace so far. Some, she knew, would already have run into the Narlaw and wouldn't make it to the palace at all.

A horrible chill swept through Dawn's body as she realized that the kingdom might really fall this time, on her watch as Palace Whisperer. She had stayed positive for so long, certain that there must be a way to overcome the Narlaw. But what if the earthstone was their only chance of survival? What if that chance was already gone?

A movement further down the track caught her attention and she peered ahead to where an old barn was visible between the tangle of trees. There was a well there, too, and a small, slight girl bent over it, lowering the bucket on its rope.

Dawn rode toward her and the girl turned, standing back from the well, looking uneasy. She couldn't have been more than six years old.

Dawn climbed down from her horse and approached the girl. "Sorry to disturb you," she said. "I'm from the palace. Have you seen a cart come this way? A grocer's cart?"

The girl shook her head. "I don't think I've seen a cart today," she said. "Most people have gone to Meridar, but we've got cows here so my father says we're staying."

She was dressed in the plain skirts and apron of a dairy farmer, but around her neck was tied a scarf of brilliant blue. It looked like silk, and the girl's hand rose toward it when she noticed Dawn looking.

"That's pretty," said Dawn. She smiled, trying to put the girl at ease.

The girl blushed. The scarf looked out of place on her – out of place in this poor, remote village. She nodded and slipped it from around her neck, holding it out to Dawn with her eyes cast down in embarrassment.

Dawn felt the luxurious smoothness of the fabric as she ran it through her fingers. She recognized the colour. All she needed was to be sure…

And there it was on the inner lining: the royal insignia and, beneath it, the initial 'O'.

"Did someone give this to you?" asked Dawn, unable to keep the urgency out of her voice.

The girl shook her head. She looked scared now.

"Don't worry," said Dawn. "You're not in trouble. It would help me a lot if you could tell me where you got it – that's all."

The girl spoke quietly, staring at the mud. "I found it in the road," she said. "Last night after leading the cows in." She pointed further along the road. "Down there by the end of the barn."

Dawn nodded. "Clever," she whispered.

It was a sign from the princess. The demon had brought her this way.

"Here." She handed the sash back to the farm girl with a smile. "You may have saved us all," she said.

The girl stared up at her, completely puzzled, but she took back the sash and clutched it tightly to her threadbare milking apron.

Dawn thanked her and rode out on to the path, staring down at the mud. There were cart tracks here, faint but readable.

She cast out into the sky, reaching for Ebony's distant presence.

Ebony! she called. *Bring Valderin. Bring everyone!*

CHAPTER 9

Rain became sleet and sleet became snow. The thin grass of the hilltop was buried in white and a layer of quiet descended.

Star slipped inside the wind shrine, snow falling in clumps from her thick fur. *It's all clear,* she whispered to Mika. *At least for a while.*

Mika nodded her thanks, but she didn't feel the relief that the news should have brought her. She sat close to the slumped, exhausted figure of Astor, watching her mentor breathe. Suri stood beside them, gently nuzzling Astor. Mika knew that the bond Astor and Suri shared was probably the only thing keeping Astor from collapsing completely.

"Why are you still here?" Astor muttered. "Your journey to the palace is everything. You mustn't wait."

Mika blinked against the onset of tears. Each time Astor spoke her heart leaped inside her. How could Mika leave her like this? It was impossible.

Star came and rested her head on Mika's knee in a silent gesture of support.

"Have I not tutored you well?" asked Astor, raising her head to look Mika in the eye. "Have I not earned your respect?"

"Of course," said Mika.

"Then why do you disobey me?"

Zabeh shifted uncomfortably where she crouched by the door. She looked restless, agitated in a way Mika had never seen before. Being struck by the elder demon must have left its mark.

"I'm not disobeying you," Mika said. "It's just that … we can't leave you here in the snow. There may be more demons…"

"You can and you will," said Astor, finding a new strength of voice. She raised a hand, gesturing to the woven shelter and the shrine above their heads. "I'll be safe here. The winds will nourish me and I do not fear the demons. My only fear is that you won't reach the Palace of the Sun. The kingdom needs you, Mika. Much more than it needs me."

Astor smiled then, and Mika felt her heart lurch once again. She looked away in case the tears she felt forming should break free.

"Zabeh," said Astor. "You will take this impudent young Whisperer away from here. Take her south-east to the river lands and on to Meridar. Do you hear me?"

Zabeh nodded, but she seemed lost in her own thoughts.

Mika felt Star stir by her side.

You know she's right, said Star. *We can't stay here – and we'd never outrun the Narlaw with Astor and Suri.*

Mika felt the urge to snap at Star, to call her selfish or disloyal, but that would be unfair. Mika knew that *she* was the one acting selfishly. Of course, she couldn't bear to think of Astor snowed in here and at the mercy of the Narlaw, but mostly she was simply afraid to go on without her. Despite her new discoveries, Mika still felt like a novice.

Mika? said Star.

She looked up and found that all eyes were watching her, awaiting her decision.

Mika nodded. "We'll go," she said.

Astor dipped her head and smiled a weary, grateful smile.

The snow continued to fall. As they left the shrine, the air was thick with it. Mika paused before she left the hilltop and turned to see the shrine almost completely obscured. Then she followed Star and Zabeh on to the hillside.

The cold in her feet and hands was matched by a numbness in her heart. She had abandoned Astor, her teacher and guardian. She placed her feet carefully on the steep, snow-encrusted path. This, she realized, was what duty felt like.

The route they had selected was a long curve that would take them close to the base of the mountains and keep them far from Rakeen. Mika squinted through the snow and struggled to tighten the drawstring at the base of her hood with her thick-gloved hands. All the while she cast around with her Whisperer sense. Did demons enjoy the cold or did they fear it? Did they feel any emotions? It was hard to imagine, considering that all they seemed to do was destroy things, feeding on the world around them. Perhaps hunger was the only thing the Narlaw could feel? If that were true, then it seemed to Mika like a terrible way to exist.

Mika trudged down off the hill, following Zabeh into a narrow cleft that offered a break from the wind. She was worried about her friend – about the effects of the Narlaw attack on her. Back at the shrine Zabeh had seemed much quieter than usual, but it was impossible to speak to her while they were caught in such a dense blizzard.

She reached instead for Star. *Don't go too far,* she whispered. *Your tracks are hard to see.*

A few moments later Star appeared in front of her. She was almost invisible in the snow. If it hadn't been for her Whisperer sense, Mika would have stepped over Star without knowing she was there.

For a while Star let Zabeh lead. She stayed alongside Mika, leaping and scampering through the deepening snow.

There's so much space, Star said. *I always forget how pure the air is outside of the city.*

Me too, said Mika, smiling at her companion's enjoyment of the snow.

It had been a long time since she, Star and Zabeh had last crept out through the smuggler's gate together. Zabeh's militia training had intensified over the last few years and she'd had less and less time to spend with Mika and Star. Mika had absorbed herself in her Whisperer training and Star had spent more time exploring the city alone. It had made Mika sad to see them drifting apart like that, and to see Star stuck in Rakeen. Despite the dire nature of their journey, Mika was glad they were together now, and glad to see her companion taking so well to her natural wildness.

The trail forks here, said Star, and she raced ahead, whipping past Zabeh's ankles.

Mika followed in Zabeh's footsteps as they

wound their way through the foothills, her boots crunching and slipping in the snow, her eyes squinting from inside her heavy woollen hood. It was exhausting work, battling the snow and wind, but there was no sense in stopping to rest until they found somewhere to shelter. Their chance came mid-afternoon when Star circled back to Mika and Zabeh on the down-slope of a riverside path. On the sheltered side of the river was a cave.

Star stood in the entrance, cautiously sniffing the air. *A bear was here,* she said, *but a long time ago.*

That's good, said Mika. *I think my feet have turned to ice. Let's rest.*

They filed inside, ducking beneath the low overhang of the entrance. It certainly did smell, but the dry rock floor and the shelter from the elements were truly welcome.

Mika sat and flipped her hood back, brushing flecks of snow from her face. Zabeh sat down opposite her, their backs to the walls of the narrow cave.

"Are you hurt?" asked Mika, nodding at a patch of reddened skin on Zabeh's cheek.

"Only from where I landed on the grass," said Zabeh. "It's nothing." She looked out to the whirling snow beyond the cave entrance.

Mika noticed her friend's eyes glisten. She had never seen Zabeh cry before.

"That demon was so strong," Zabeh added in a rush. "I felt its power when it struck me, like a deep void desperate to engulf me... I..."

Mika reached out a hand and placed it on Zabeh's knee. "I felt it, too," she said, "but it's gone now."

Zabeh turned to her. "I thought I was brave," she said, "but when I fell to the ground I was too scared to get back up." She looked down at the cracked stone floor. Her right hand lay limp on the hilt of her sword.

"You *are* brave," said Mika. "You stood your ground, but nobody can fight a demon like that without the power of the earth behind them."

Speaking those words made Mika shudder. She still couldn't believe she and Astor had actually managed to banish the demon.

"But you fought it," said Zabeh. "You destroyed it."

There was a light of admiration in Zabeh's eyes. Mika tried to dismiss it with an embarrassed shake of her head, but Zabeh held her gaze. She was serious.

They had been friends all their lives. Mika was the careful one, the studious one, and Zabeh was the fearless warrior. It was a new sensation, for Mika to be viewed as a warrior.

Mika smiled at her friend. "Think of it as payback for all the times you've saved me," she said.

Zabeh smiled back, wiping her damp eyes on the sleeve of her coat. "That has happened quite a lot," she said.

"Remember when those boys threw rotten fish-heads at me from their river boat?" said Mika. "You gathered up everything they'd thrown – plus some extra dirt from the street – and dumped it back on their heads when they passed under the rice-market bridge."

Zabeh laughed. "Half of it ended up on the old man who was steering the boat. He wasn't very impressed."

Mika unwrapped her food pack and they ate a

small meal – half a rice cake each and some thin slices of pickled radish. They chatted about all the times Zabeh had got them both into trouble, then somehow got them out of it again. The wind howled outside and Star climbed into Mika's lap, watching the cave entrance. Her nose twitched, wary of the bear's return.

When the meal was over they reluctantly set off into the snow.

Mika walked ahead of Zabeh this time, straining to make out Star's darting movements as she nosed out the trail. The visibility was so poor it was like passing through a tunnel. Mika's feet grew increasingly damp and cold as water seeped through her trousers and trickled into her boots. Huge snowflakes landed on her exposed cheeks and, when she brushed them away, more snow was left there by her gloves. But she felt no sign of the Narlaw and, as she walked, she continued to hope that Astor was safe.

The sky grew dim as evening approached and Star rushed madly to and fro, darting off the path at every opportunity to find them shelter for the night. When she finally settled at Mika's side, the bond between them pulsed with satisfaction.

A shepherd's hut, she said. *Not far.*

Good news, said Mika, smiling at Star's enthusiasm.

Soon she and Zabeh were shovelling snow from the front of the shack's wooden door, using their hands and feet in the failing light.

Inside were two long benches and a storm lamp. There was nowhere to make a fire, but the lamp gave out some heat and the three of them huddled together, warming their frozen hands and paws. Mika brushed the melting snow off Star's back, and Star shook herself out with a gruff noise that was half bark and half sneeze.

They ate, saving as much as they could for the next day's travel, then settled in for their first, cold night in the wilds.

The morning brought a clear sky and a rare view of the country around them.

Mika climbed on to a flat boulder beside the

hut, dislodging a layer of snow. The highlands rolled away north, snow-dusted and shining in the morning light. Rakeen was a dark smudge in the middle distance. They had come further than Mika had realized. Eight or ten miles perhaps. Mika swung round to face the south. Mountains rose to impossible heights on her right, white and purple, their peaks unknowable, visited only by eagles and other birds.

Away down this jagged line of mountains lay the plunging valleys of the river lands, the gateway from the highlands into central Meridina.

Mika allowed herself one last, long look to the north. The wind shrine was lost in the distance now. Mika closed her eyes and sent a final wish of safety and farewell to Astor.

They walked without rest until noon, and then they only paused long enough to catch their breath and take a few quick mouthfuls of food.

In the foothills they passed abandoned homes and hill stations, barracks for patrolling militia and several wind shrines. They descended gradually, and the ground showed through in patches where the snows of the previous day had failed to take hold. Much of this ground was bare where Mika would have expected to see grass. There were noticeable gaps in the thorny trees that studded the hillsides, too – scars left by the Narlaw.

An hour before dusk Star scampered up the steep side of the gully they were hiking through and peered to the south-east.

There it is! she said. *The mirror lake.*

Mika watched her companion dart along the lip of the gully. She watched Zabeh up ahead, too. Her friend turned the next corner in the path and stopped, hands on her hips.

Mika ran to catch up. Around the bend the gully dipped into open land, the mountains drew back and there, spread before them, was the shimmering expanse of the mirror lake, its shores lined with cairns and standing stones. A wind shrine stood on the lake's south-eastern shore and, beyond, the land fell into a plunging river valley. There lay the heartland of the kingdom and the Meridar road.

CHAPTER 10

They walked until the light gave out and then they set up camp beside the river. An old fire pit lay in the centre of a flat patch of grass about twenty paces wide. A steep rocky slope rose on three sides, protecting this notch of land from the wind.

They would have to cross the river eventually to reach the Meridar road, but the two bridges they had passed so far had both been destroyed. On the opposite side of the river, the devastation left by the Narlaw was much more severe: hillsides turned to mud, trees torn into splinters. Mika wondered if the bridges had been broken by the demons or by survivors from this side. She had felt the presence of people, distantly, as they had descended the valley – locals hiding from the Narlaw, she presumed.

After collecting firewood they settled in for the night, Mika staring into the crackling flames and revelling in their heat. Star sat close beside her. Her snow-wet fur steamed as it dried and her ears twitched as she listened to the sounds of the night. Mika kept watch over Zabeh, who sat, exhausted and silent, by her side, but soon the fire began to lull Mika toward sleep.

Then she saw Star rise quickly to her feet, and felt the first tell-tale signs of movement at the edge of her senses.

"Demons?" asked Zabeh, suddenly alert.

"No," said Mika. "People."

They're on the river path, said Star. *Coming north, this way.*

Mika reached out and sensed a group of seven riders on horseback. "Why would anyone be travelling north?" she said.

Zabeh cast her a worried look. "Should we go?" she asked. She had loosened her sword in its scabbard and was peering north up the river trail, their only escape route.

"They've got horses," Mika said. "I don't think we could get away." She looked over at her friend. "They may be able to help us cross the river," she said.

Zabeh nodded, and the three of them stood side by side with their backs to the fire.

The first of the riders rounded the bend – a man with long grey-streaked hair and a shaggy beard. "Ho!" he shouted, reining in his horse. "Good night to you."

Mika peered through the gloom as the others arrived behind him. They were a tough, tired-looking group, each of them wrapped up in makeshift clothing that suggested they were not used to travelling in snow. Mika watched the riders closely as they approached the camp fire. Most of their faces were still deep in shadow.

"We saw the light from your fire," said the bearded man, who appeared to be their leader. "There aren't too many travellers in these parts. Are you running from the demons, too?"

Firelight flickered over his face. He sat casually in his saddle and smiled.

Mika felt Star's wariness and Zabeh's body language was equally tense.

"We're heading for Meridar," said Mika. She didn't know if she should be speaking to these people at all, but she had to say something. "Rakeen was overrun by the Narlaw."

The man responded with a sombre nod. He glanced down at Star, and Mika noticed him share a look with a woman rider who had drawn up beside him. The woman also nodded, but not at what Mika had said. There was an arrogance to her manner and the way she stared at Star made Mika feel nervous.

I don't like these people, Star said.

Me neither, whispered Mika. She glanced sideways and saw Zabeh narrow her eyes. Her friend still had a hand on her sword hilt.

The riders at the back of the group began to move, slowly circling around the fire to stand their horses behind Mika, Star and Zabeh. No one spoke for several moments and the only sounds were the crackle and spit of the fire, and the thud of the stepping horses.

The lead rider broke the silence. "I suppose I should tell you," he said, "that we came here looking for a Whisperer."

The woman next to him peered down at Mika and Star with an unpleasant grin. "Looks like we found one," she said.

Zabeh stepped forwards. "And what would you want with a Whisperer?" she demanded. "Are you thieves?"

The woman rider laughed and the bearded man simply watched them with lazy, confident eyes. "Not thieves," the man said, "but there's money to be made if we can hand over your friend here."

Mika's heart began to pound in her chest. "Over to whom?" she asked.

The man's eyes narrowed. "You'll find out soon enough," he said.

Mika's mind raced. Who could possibly be offering money for kidnapped Whisperers? Then the answer was suddenly clear. "The Narlaw," she said. A hollow feeling took hold of her. It seemed impossible, yet she knew instinctively that it was true.

"Clever girl," the man said. "Let's see if you're clever enough to come quietly."

Zabeh drew her sword in direct response. "Traitors!" she said. "You'd sell your own kingdom for a piece of gold?"

"The world has changed," said the man. "Call us traitors if you like, but we're the ones who'll survive this war. We've chosen the right side. That's all."

Mika could see her friend's hands were shaking. She felt her own body tense uncontrollably. How could this be happening?

We have to run, said Star.

There's nowhere to run to, said Mika. *They have horses. They'll chase us down in seconds.*

But then a thought came to her. Mika reached out carefully to the huge, docile presences of the horses. If they couldn't run from the horses, maybe she could make the horses run from them?

The leader swung out of his saddle and stepped toward them. "Put the sword down, girl," he said to Zabeh. "Don't be a fool." He swept a hand out to take in the other tough-looking men and women.

"Just give up and you won't be hurt."

Zabeh switched swordhands and moved into a defensive stance, Star bristled with fear and anger at Mika's side, and Mika reached out swiftly to the horse that now stood riderless behind the gang's leader.

She knew how suggestible a horse could be, and how often they were driven by fear. It was unkind to the animal, but this was her only chance – she sent the image of a snarling bear into the horse's mind.

Right away the horse whinnied and bolted forwards, nudging its rider and charging past the fire toward the rest of the gang.

The other horses began to rear and snort as Mika sent them startling images, one by one.

The leader of the gang stood, confused for a moment, then glared at Mika and strode toward her in a rage. "That's enough from you, Whisperer! You're coming with me!"

Star ran at him, snarling. She dodged a kick from his boot and leaped for his forearm, but the man was strong. He shoved Star away and sent her scrambling across the grass.

Star! cried Mika.

Run, Mika! Star called back. *Down the river path!*

But the man was already upon her. He grabbed the hood of Mika's coat as she tried to dart away and pulled her back viciously, forcing a choked gasp from her throat.

"Mika!" Zabeh cried. She swung her sword in a wide arc and the traitors who had closed around her leaped back. She burst past them toward her friend.

The leader turned as Zabeh came for him. He let go of Mika's hood and dived away, rolling to avoid the swing of Zabeh's sword.

Mika stood, clutching her throat. The horses thumped manically around them, still darting about in fear. Their shadows swept around the camp.

"You have to go!" hissed Zabeh.

Come on! urged Star.

The leader of the gang rose to his feet and Zabeh made a warning thrust with her sword. He backed away, but another man crashed into Zabeh from behind. Her sword flew from her hand and more of the attackers rushed in to pin her to the ground.

"Run!" Zabeh called to Mika as she struggled. "You can still make it!"

Mika glanced around in a panic. She saw an opening. If she could reach the river path, she and Star could get help. But that would mean leaving Zabeh to fight alone.

So Mika charged with Star by her side and crashed, screaming, into the traitors who had captured her friend. She swung her fists and grabbed at arms and legs as she tried to pull Zabeh free.

Something struck her in the side of the head and she fell to the ground. She heard Star snarling, the angry cries of men and women and, somewhere in there, Zabeh's frustrated, desperate voice.

Mika felt herself lifted from the grass. She struggled and kicked out, but she was still dazed from the blow to her head. Her arms were bent back and held painfully behind her. She heard Star snarl and then whimper somewhere close by.

Star! she cried. *Star!*

Then she felt herself being draped over the huge back of one of the horses. From there she saw the river, glimmering and black, a few paces away.

Again, Star snarled, trying to reach Mika, but this time a splash followed.

Mika saw a flash of white fur as Star was thrown into the river.

"No!" she cried. She used all her strength to kick and squirm against her attackers, but her arms were being tied behind her back. She couldn't get free.

Star! she called, again and again, as her companion was swept away by the cold, fast currents of the river.

CHAPTER 11

Mika lay with her wrists and ankles tied, draped over the horse's dappled grey back as if she were a sack of grain. Her muscles ached and every step the horse took sent a fresh jolt of pain through her body. The smell of horse sweat and saddle leather filled her nostrils, and the boots of the gang's leader hung to her right as he steered them down the winding path.

The river rushed and gurgled nearby and Mika's thoughts returned again and again to Star. She had lost her companion. She couldn't feel her, couldn't hope to hear Star's whispers in her head. Star could swim, but in a river so fast and cold…

Mika couldn't bear to think about what might have happened.

She could feel Zabeh's presence a few horses back and the knowledge that she was not alone was the only thing that kept Mika from losing hope, but the awful fear of their destination hovered ominously. She and Zabeh were to be sold like livestock to the demons.

And then what? Would it be the ghost-sleep? Or worse?

No Whisperer caught by the Narlaw would be treated kindly.

Mika felt more scared now than she ever had – even after all she had seen and done since the Narlaw came. She was powerless against these human traitors. They couldn't be banished like a demon could. Her only idea was to spook the horses into bolting again, but that was simply too dangerous now she and Zabeh were tied to their backs. There was nothing she could do but wait.

Mika winced as the horse broke into a trot and its joints thumped into her stomach and chest. She was glad Astor couldn't see her like this – captured before she'd even made it to the Meridar road.

Some time during the night, Mika fell into an exhausted kind of half-sleep. She closed her eyes and felt her body grow gradually numb to the pain of the horseback ride. Although true rest was impossible, she was able to quiet her thoughts, to find some small relief from the fear that clung to her.

Was she giving up? No, she told herself. When she reached the Narlaw she would fight with everything she had. She would banish as many as she could with the fury she had felt back in Rakeen. She knew there would be too many demons to overcome – a whole army of them, perhaps – but she would fight until the very end. With that thought in mind, she let herself drift, as the traitor's horse carried her away.

Mika jolted awake.

Icy water splashed into her face. She flinched, pulling her head up and feeling a sharp spasm of pain across her back and arms.

They were crossing the river. The water rushed and eddied around them and the horse's hooves clacked and slipped on the rocky river bed. Mika lurched in her bindings and for an instant she thought she would fall head first into the waters, but the ropes held her fast to the big horse's back.

She shook the drops of water from her face and tried to look about. A silvery sheen lay over the water – the first light of morning had arrived.

As they clambered up the river bank, Mika's abductor pulled his horse around.

"A straight line east from here," he said as others in the group rode up beside him.

Mika couldn't see any of them from her position – and she didn't want to. They had sided with an army of demons that sought to destroy the whole of Meridina. She couldn't imagine a worse act of treachery. Nor could she imagine what they hoped to do with the gold they were paid for her capture. What use was gold in a world with no crops left to eat? With no other people left to buy from or speak to?

The leader spun his horse around and Mika strained to take in her surroundings. For a giddy instant she caught sight of Zabeh, bound behind a woman's saddle and peering right back at her. Their eyes met, but there was no time to speak. The horses moved back into a single file and Zabeh was gone from sight, but Mika had seen the anger and determination in her friend's eyes. The same feelings burned inside her, too. She strained against the ropes tying her down, growling in frustration as the horses set off at a painful canter. No matter how hard she tried, she couldn't loosen the ropes. She could do nothing but hold on and save her strength for the Narlaw.

As the sun rose, they left the river behind and set out on to the green flatlands of central Meridina. Mika watched the grass flick by beneath the horse's powerful legs. They were heading east like the leader of the group had said. More and more often they crossed areas of ruined earth, signs that the Narlaw had passed this way in great numbers. Mika strained to catch sight of Zabeh, but it seemed they were deliberately being kept apart. Once again she thought about making her and Zabeh's horses bolt. Perhaps the riders would be thrown and she and Zabeh would survive through being tied to the horses. Or perhaps she and Zabeh would end up beneath the horses' hooves or lying in the grass with broken bones.

At mid-morning they passed through the shattered remnants of a town. Almost every building had lost its roof. There were signs of fire and the demon sickness lingered over everything, turning Mika's stomach. They had to be drawing near to the demon army now, she thought. Mika suppressed the urge to panic as she was carried through the empty streets of the town. Instead, she found herself becoming strangely calm – ready to accept her fate and do her best at banishing the Narlaw.

It was in this state of calm that Mika heard her name spoken. At first she thought it was Zabeh calling for her. She craned her neck painfully to look for her friend, but saw only the cruel, weary face of the rider directly behind her. Then, when she heard her name again, she realized who it was.

Mika. Her heart leaped. *Mika, can you hear me?*

Yes, said Mika. *Where are you?*

She reached out and felt Star's warm, vital presence. It was the greatest thing she had ever felt.

We're over the ridge to the north, said Star. *Can you get away from the horses?*

No, said Mika. *We're tied to them.*

Well, said Star. *Just try to keep your heads down.*

That won't be hard, said Mika, letting her face rest against the clammy flanks of the horse.

She sensed two people and two horses beyond the ridge – Star had brought help. Mika thought about warning Zabeh, but that would only alert the traitors, too. Instead she concentrated on Star's presence, letting hope kindle inside her for the first time since she had been taken.

They continued away from the town, parallel to the low ridge where Star was waiting. Mika held her breath in anticipation. Who had Star brought with her and what were they planning?

Then there was a horrible cry from further back in the line of riders.

The horse carrying Mika stopped as the leader of the group turned to look. Mika glimpsed a man on the ground and his horse standing riderless. The shaft of an arrow slanted from the centre of the fallen man's back.

Another arrow flew. This time it thudded into the ground and several of the riders wheeled their horses away and fled at a gallop.

Keep low, whispered Star. *We're coming for you.*

The leader yelled, "It's an ambush! Ride!" and he kicked the horse into a gallop.

Mika bounced behind the saddle, winded and gasping for breath. She twisted her head and saw two riders crest the ridge to the north. One moved slowly, upright with a bow in their hands. The other galloped down on a course to intercept Mika's horse.

Another scream came from the panicked ranks of the traitors. Mika tried to see what was going on, to see if Zabeh was all right, but everything was a blur. The thunder of hooves drowned out all other sounds. Mika tensed her muscles, hoping that the ropes would hold and she wouldn't be thrown from the horse.

In the saddle, the leader of the traitors kicked and shouted at his horse to go faster. But in no time at all there was another horse alongside them.

Mika.

She craned her neck and saw Star riding at the pommel of the other horse's saddle. Holding the reins was Jen.

She had made it! The warriors had made it out of Rakeen.

There were only two of them, but Mika didn't have time to think about what had happened to the others. As soon as Jen had her horse close enough, she drew her sword and struck out at Mika's captor.

The man dodged the blow and the horse swerved, whinnying in pain at the man yanking the reins. Mika swung and thumped against its flanks. The gap widened between the two horses and she realized that Jen must have ridden her horse to near exhaustion to have caught up with them.

Don't worry, said Star, sensing Mika's fear. *I won't lose you again.*

Mika glanced across and saw Star balanced on Jen's lap, ready to jump.

She leaped across and the traitor cried out in surprise. Mika couldn't see, but Star must have tackled the rider because the horse suddenly lost control. An instant later the man screamed and fell from the horse. Mika saw a white blur on the ground with him as the horse galloped away.

Star! she called.

She saw Star back away from the fallen man, who lay clutching his leg and writhing in pain.

Jen drew alongside and reined in the runaway horse. "Here," she said, as she stopped the horses and leaned in to cut the ropes.

Mika slid down into Jen's arms. She could barely stand, her muscles ached so badly.

And then Star was with her, leaping into her arms. Mika dropped into the swaying grass and held her companion close, overwhelmed with relief, exhaustion and gratitude.

They left the injured traitors where they lay, taking their horses. Mika and Zabeh rode side by side.

"I don't know about you," said Zabeh, "but I don't feel sorry for them at all."

Mika shook her head. "Me neither. What kind of person would trade the safety of their own kingdom for a piece of gold?"

Zabeh remained quiet for a moment, staring at the pommel of her saddle. Then she looked across at Mika. "Thanks for not leaving me," she said, "at the campfire. You were brave. Stupid, but brave." She smiled.

"You wouldn't have left me, either," said Mika.

Slowly they departed from the scene of the fight. Three of the traitors had fled and two others had been killed. One of the casualties was the woman carrying Zabeh. She had put up quite a fight, but the other Rakeen warrior, Damon, had beaten her in combat and rescued Zabeh.

As they set out north-east, riding toward

Meridar, Jen and Damon spoke of their escape from Rakeen. Mika listened closely to the sad tale of Guran and the others. They had given their lives so she could carry her secret to Meridar. Although she couldn't help feeling guilty, she knew that the real blame lay with the Narlaw alone. She had to make this journey worthwhile. She had to reach Meridar and teach the other Whisperers how to reverse the ghost-sleep and banish the Narlaw for good.

The morning sun fell bright and unflinching on the devastated countryside. Mika stroked Star and glanced across at Zabeh, who looked as bruised and exhausted as Mika was.

We'll be in Meridar soon, said Star.

Mika smiled. *There's still a long ride ahead. Maybe now you can tell me how you got out of that river and found the others?*

Star looked up at her mischievously. *A wild fox can escape from any dangerous situation,* she said. *You wouldn't understand.*

You mean Jen and Damon found you, then?

Star settled back on to the front of the saddle.

They might have noticed me drying off on the eastern bank of the river. I was sneezing quite a lot.

Mika laughed. *Well, I'm glad you found us,* she said. *You saved our lives.*

And now we're together, said Star, *there's nothing that can stop us.*

Mika nodded, and felt in her bones that Star was absolutely right.

CHAPTER 12

Princess Ona sat up with a jolt.

The cart had stopped. Somehow she had slept, but now that her eyes were open, darkness crowded in on her and the realization of where she was returned with a chilling rush of fear.

More than three days had passed since she had been spirited out of the palace by the demon masquerading as Captain Niels. Her abandoned blue sash had led to nothing. The only sign that anyone might have been searching for her was the slow, cautious progress of her prison-cart. The roads they were travelling had become bumpier and more crooked by the mile. It seemed her captor was still taking pains to avoid being seen.

Occasionally, the cart had stopped and, with a

growled warning, the demon had unlocked the back doors and thrown some bread in for Ona to eat. She had been allowed out of the cart only twice. Each time she had stumbled into the light, finding herself in the midst of dense woodland with the demon pointing her toward a nearby stream or brook. Ona was so thirsty and weak by then that escape was impossible. Instead, she drank greedily and washed her face and hands in the flowing water before returning to her moving prison.

When the cart doors opened for a third time, Ona was greeted by darkness outside. She grasped the earthstone and stared, wide-eyed, at the shadowy form of her captor.

"Out," said the demon. Its voice was harsh and dry. Its posture was unnaturally upright – a tall silhouette against the dusky sky. "Out," it growled again. "Now."

Ona slid forwards cautiously on her knees. With the doors open she heard the swish of trees and the snort of the cart-horse. As she neared the door she heard footsteps. Her heart skipped – they had reached the other Narlaw. It was over. She closed her eyes, wanting to weep, but the demon's voice broke in on her.

"Hurry up, or I'll drag you out."

Ona stepped down on to soft earth. Her legs were weak from being cramped for so long. Voices echoed, drawing nearer, and Ona took a deep breath.

"Now," she whispered to herself. She thrust the earthstone toward the shadowy face of the demon and, as it shrank back in horror, Ona turned and ran.

Her shoes sank into the mud. She felt heavy and slow and the cold evening air stung her throat.

Seconds later something crashed into her from behind and she fell on her face. Hands grasped her by the shoulders and turned her over. She fumbled for the earthstone, shoving it at her attacker. But the face she saw wasn't that of Captain Niels. It was dirty, unshaven and lank-haired and it didn't flinch at all from the earthstone. Ona gasped in shock. This was a man, not a demon.

The man laughed and Ona turned her face from his stinking breath.

"That necklace won't work on me," the man said. He laughed again as he lifted Ona easily off the floor.

Mud clung to her face and made her dress stick to her body. She tried to shake free of the man, but he was twice her size.

The demon-Niels watched as Ona was dragged back toward it. "Take her inside," it said.

Ona was pushed off the road and on to a footpath, through trees that hissed in the wind.

"Where are you taking me?" she cried. "Don't you know that was a demon? A Narlaw?"

"You're kidding me?" said the man in mock surprise. "A demon? Well I never." He laughed again, shoving Ona ahead of him along the path.

She stumbled through the trees until the lights of a building became visible ahead. The woods ended in a clearing and Ona was confronted by an inn. Its signboard swayed and shadows passed across its lamplit windows.

Panic rose up and made Ona's breathing frantic. She wanted to go home to the palace, to her father and Yusuf and all of her friends. Was this her final destination? She thought she was being taken to the Narlaw army. But maybe the demons planned to lock her up here, in the middle of nowhere, where no one would ever find her. The wind seemed to blast right through her, making her shiver uncontrollably as she crossed the clearing. The man thrust her toward a low doorway and the stale, mildew smell of the inn.

Inside a dozen pairs of eyes turned to regard her. Ona froze at the edge of the long, low-ceilinged room. Tobacco smoke hung above the heads of the men and women of the inn, mixing unpleasantly with the odour of stale beer and unwashed bodies. The princess scanned the room with growing terror. The faces that looked back at her were shrewd and suspicious. She knew that some must be demons – the ones with blank expressions, the ones who barely seemed to breathe as they watched her. The others would be the kind of desperate criminals she had heard tales about as a small child. Who else would be so low as to associate with the Narlaw?

The door banged behind her and Ona turned to see the demon-Niels glaring with a thin smile on its face.

"You," it said, nodding at the man who had brought Ona inside. "Take the necklace from her."

"No!" cried Ona.

But the man grabbed the whole thing and tore it from around her neck, jerking her forwards painfully.

Ona reached for the back of her neck where the clasp had broken.

"What are you going to do to me?" she muttered, summoning the courage to look Niels in the eye.

"I think we'll keep you a little longer," it said. "The king may be persuaded to surrender his armies once he knows who has his precious daughter."

"He won't," said Ona. "And anyway, the Whisperers will fight you to the end. They'll banish you just like Queen Amina—"

"Quiet." The demon advanced on her. "Take her away," it ordered a tall, fair-haired man. "You," it said to another, "hide the cart."

"Where are you taking me?" Ona cried. "Please!"

But no one was listening.

The blond man guided her toward the door. "Don't make a fuss," he said. "It'll be a lot easier that way."

Ona walked ahead of him obediently, out into the wind-blown night and across a short stretch of mud toward the stables. All hope had drained from her. They had the earthstone and she had no protection. No one had come to save her.

She entered the stables and the man began tightening the saddle of his horse. A pair of lamps hung from the ceiling and Ona counted thirteen horses in total. She watched him wrestle with his horse's saddle. He looked strong and she knew there was no chance of outrunning him. But there was an uncertainty in his manner – it was almost as if he was embarrassed by what he was doing.

The man looked up and saw Ona watching him. "Don't get any ideas," he said. "There's nowhere to run to. Even if you made it into the woods, those demons would find you in a heartbeat." He tightened the strap and slipped a buckle into place beneath the horse's belly. "Nothing you can do," he said.

"What about you?" said Ona.

The man looked at her, puzzled.

"You could help me," she said.

The man narrowed his eyes at her and shook his head. "It's best you stop talking."

Ona felt desperation rise up inside her. She'd felt nothing but fear, hunger and exhaustion for three days and now she would be sent to the Narlaw army. Beyond any chance of rescue. This man was her last hope. There was a softness in him – she could see it in the way he barely looked at her. And he wasn't drunk like most of the others had seemed.

"Do you know who I am?" Ona asked.

The man ignored her.

"My father is the king," she said. "He would pay you much more than the demons are. More than you can imagine. I'd say you rescued me. If we ride north now we could be gone before they—"

"We'd be dead," the man said, finally turning to face her. "They'd catch us. I've seen them move. I've seen them hunt. And your father doesn't have enough gold to bring us back to life, does he? Can the king turn back time? Can he go back and stop the demons invading, stop them destroying my farm and turning my wife into a living corpse? I couldn't make it north to hide behind the walls of Meridar and neither could my son or daughter. The demons surrounded the market town. They offered protection to anyone who would volunteer. The rest they put to sleep." His eyes flashed with the horror of that memory. "My children are waiting for me," he said. "So, you should save your breath. I'll be finishing the job I came here for."

He turned his back on Ona and shook the saddle, making sure it was steady.

"Do you really want to live in a world of demons?" Ona asked, her voice rising in anger. "Do you really think you and your family will be set free after the Narlaw have overrun the entire kingdom? They took your wife. The only way to bring her back is to defeat the Narlaw once and for all."

The man flinched and then peered at her sideways as he stroked his horse's neck.

"Help me take the earthstone back to Meridar," whispered Ona. "You can save everyone. You can wake your wife from the ghost-sleep."

The man stared into a dark corner of the stables. Outside, the wind rippled through the woods and creaked the building's old wooden frame.

"You're lying," the man said.

"I swear," said Ona, taking a step toward him. "I swear it's true. The necklace they took from me has the power to win this war."

The man shook his head. "Even if I could get my hands on it –" Ona's heart lurched with a sudden surge of hope – "Even if we could get away from here unseen," the man said. "They would track us down. We wouldn't stand a chance."

The stable door creaked loudly and Ona spun to see the demon-Niels standing tall and still in the doorway.

"You wouldn't stand a chance at what?" it said.

Ona backed away. She glanced behind her and saw the man's jaw working uselessly, searching in vain for a way out.

Two other figures appeared behind the demon in the doorway. Niels stepped inside and the other two demons followed, their blank eyes boring into Ona as she stared back at them in horror.

"It seems we need a new rider," said Niels. It strode past the princess and up to the man.

"Wait…" the man spluttered.

But Niels placed a hand on his forehead and the man crumpled to the ground. Then the demon turned to Ona.

"Please," she whimpered. "No."

"I think it's best you sleep the rest of the way," the demon said, reaching a hand toward Ona's head.

She stumbled back into the warm flank of the horse. The horse snorted and edged away. She screamed as the demon laid its cold, open palm on her forehead and she felt a terrible, sickening rush.

Her vision blurred and everything turned to black.

CHAPTER 13

It was Ebony who found the cart. She swooped out of the pitch black night and nearly scared Dawn's horse into bolting.

There's a tavern in the woods! she said. *Two minutes' ride from here. It's empty, but there's a cart in the stable block that reeks of Narlaw.*

Take us there! said Dawn. She raised her torch and nudged her horse into a canter, away from the tracks she and the guards had been following.

The inn was dark and silent amid the trees, but as soon as Dawn drew near she felt the recent presence of demons. She dismounted and stepped inside. From the way the chairs and tables had been moved around, she could see that a large group had made this place their own.

How far behind are we? she asked Ebony.

Ebony hopped across the floor, her black feathers shining in the flickering light of Dawn's torch. *I'd guess less than an hour,* she said. *The demons' scent is fresh.*

Then we can still catch them, said Dawn. She stared at Ebony, and knew her companion would be thinking the same as she was – the demon had joined up with others. Lots of others.

Valderin ducked into the tavern. "Fresh horse tracks on the road," he said. "Twelve at least, all heading south."

Dawn nodded. A dozen Narlaw meant she and the palace guards would be outnumbered if it came to a fight, which it certainly would. The demons wouldn't let Princess Ona or the earthstone go easily.

"Let's go," she said.

She strode out to where the other six guards awaited their orders.

Can you lead us to the Narlaw? she asked Ebony.

You follow the tracks, said Ebony. *I'll go ahead and try to sniff them out.*

Right, said Dawn. She swung back on to her horse and Ebony launched into the air above her.

They rode hard.

Dawn and Valderin led, side by side, Dawn holding tight to the reins and listening for Ebony's voice above the thunder of hooves. They had put out their torches to keep their approach a surprise.

The thin woods gave way to meadows and Dawn felt the night around her, cold and charged with fear.

Any sign? she called to Ebony.

No, but I can feel them. We're closing in.

Dawn prepared her mind for the battle ahead. She had only faced one demon at a time before and hadn't always come off best. This time there could be as many as twelve. She breathed deeply, drawing the cool air into her body and reaching out into the passing night with her Whisperer sense. She felt the earth embrace her. She would need its help if she was to rescue Ona and the earthstone.

I can see them! cried Ebony. *They're at the edge of a ruined town about two hundred paces away. Off the main road.*

Dawn shouted these directions across to Valderin, who drew his sword as a signal to his guards. Across the meadow, Dawn spotted the outlines of buildings, just visible against the dark horizon. She raced toward them, swerving off the main road on to a rutted track.

I can see the princess, Ebony said.

Dawn's heart skipped.

She's near the back of the group, said Ebony. *Unconscious, I think. It's a man riding the horse, not a demon. Half of the group are humans.*

Humans? said Dawn. *But why?*

Then she realized. The demons needed people to carry the earthstone. She wondered, bitterly, how much these people were being paid.

They haven't spotted us yet, said Ebony. *If you skirt the southern edge of the town you'll be on them in no time.*

Thanks, Dawn whispered. *Try not to get too close. They might sense you.*

Understood, said Ebony.

Dawn felt her companion circle back, gliding

above her, unseen in the night sky.

They reached the edge of the town in what felt like a heartbeat. All the thatch was gone from the roofs, and the cottages, shops and barns stood silent and empty of life. It was one of the towns the Narlaw had destroyed on their way to the city of Altenheim.

Dawn squinted against the rush of cold air as she galloped her horse past the edge of the town. If they failed to rescue Ona and the earthstone now, these demons would soon join up with the rest of their kind and all would be lost.

She closed her eyes for a moment and reached out. Right away she felt the demons ahead. They were close. Dawn opened her eyes. It was hard to see anything with the wind so strong in her face, but she thought, just for a second, that she had spotted them.

Yes, said Ebony. *Get ready.*

Dawn turned to face Valderin, whose horse thundered beside her. She pointed to the vague silhouettes ahead in the grass and Valderin nodded.

He raised his sword hand. "Guards!" he cried. "Charge!"

177

They manoeuvred into an arrowhead formation with Valderin and Dawn at its point.

Dawn stared ahead with wide eyes. A shout flew to her on the wind, then more cries rang out. The last of the town flashed by to her left and they sped into open country.

Then, in the long grass of the meadow, the guards and the Narlaw collided.

Dawn reached instantly for the first demon she could feel. It was still riding away and Dawn's blood was so alive from the chase that she barely flinched at the sickness brought on by the Narlaw's presence. She felt the demon swerve on its horse, felt its attempt to fight back, pushing against her grip. But the earth surged through her and the demon was wrenched from the world.

Dawn watched the riderless horse stumble and fall. The horse behind crashed into it and its rider also tumbled to the ground.

It was then Dawn saw Ona, falling like a rag doll beside him.

The fallen rider rose to his feet and turned to

face the thundering guards. He stood beside the crumpled form of Princess Ona and drew a pair of axes from his back. Two other riders, both men, had also stopped and turned their horses to fight.

Valderin charged ahead, closing the ground in seconds, and he and the axe-man swung at each other as Valderin passed.

Dawn veered away from the collision and heard metal slither and clang as the riders crashed into each other. She swerved round, slowing her horse and glancing across to where the princess lay.

The axe-man remained standing beside her, but there was a strange, incredulous look on his grizzled features. He took a step toward Dawn then collapsed. He lay on the ground, unmoving.

Dawn nudged her horse into action and, as they drew near, she saw the wound Valderin had inflicted on his first pass. The man was dead.

Dawn leaped from her saddle and ran to Ona's side.

Is she breathing? Ebony asked, circling above the battle.

Dawn cupped the princess's head in her hands and felt her neck for a pulse. She reached for Ona with her Whisperer sense, too, but it was just as she had feared.

The ghost-sleep, she said.

Dawn cradled the princess in her arms and stared out at the chaos of the fight. She felt like crying.

At least she's alive, said Ebony. *We can take her back to the palace. When the war is over, she'll wake.*

Yes, said Dawn bitterly. *All we have to do is banish every single Narlaw in the kingdom.*

A thought struck her and she quickly fumbled to check the princess's neck.

The necklace was gone. Of course it was. The earthstone would be up ahead with the fastest riders, guarded by Narlaw and on its way to the demon army.

Dawn bowed her head in disappointment and exhaustion. Then she lay Ona's head down gently and rose to her feet.

What can you see? she asked Ebony.

Ebony flapped higher, over the battleground.

Four riders have escaped to the south. Moving fast.

That's where the earthstone is, said Dawn. *We have to go after it. One of the guards can look after the princess.*

But before she could get Valderin's attention, the battle was upon her.

"Fall back!" cried Valderin.

Dawn watched in horror as one of Valderin's guards was flung into the air, landing with a sickening thud some twenty paces across the meadow.

Horses thumped toward her and she recognized Valderin and two of his guards. Were they the only ones left?

Behind them came the demons – two of them – eyes aglow, moving low to the ground and horribly fast.

Dawn reached for them both, but she was tired and disorientated. She couldn't hold on to the earth trance. She let go, her head spinning, then tried again, this time grasping only one of the demons.

As she felt the earth flow through her, she heard Valderin and his guards renew the fight. She focused all of her anger on the demon in her grip and held on tightly as her body rushed with the banishing power of the earth.

The demon was torn away and Dawn looked up to see Valderin towering over her on his horse. The final demon leaped at him and Dawn stumbled back as Valderin's horse swung round manically, almost trampling her. She fell to the ground beside the sleeping princess and cast out desperately at the last remaining demon.

Its presence clashed against her as she fought to hold on to it.

But Dawn was also strong. And she was angry. With a wordless cry she channelled the cleansing power of the earth. The demon shrieked and was gone, cast back into the Darklands.

Dawn sat on the cold grass, dizzy and sick.

Ebony had arrived beside her and was watching her closely. *Can you stand?* she asked.

I think so.

Can you ride? Ebony asked.

I'll have to, said Dawn.

She looked around. The dead axe-man lay an arm's reach from her. One of Valderin's guards lay flat on his back, barely alive. Only Valderin and one other guard had survived the battle unscathed, but they both sat slumped on their horses as if they were about to drop.

"The earthstone is gone," said Dawn. "They fled with it as soon as they saw us."

Valderin looked down wearily from his mount. He nodded. "Then we'll go after them," he said. "Here." He held out a gauntleted hand and Dawn reached up to take it.

But as she rose there was a sharp snick and a thud and Valderin's grip faltered.

Dawn looked up as the captain doubled over with a groan and slid from his saddle. "No!" she cried, trying to catch him as he fell, but he was far too heavy and he tumbled through Dawn's arms and on to the ground. Dawn dropped to her knees. "Captain?" she said. "Captain?"

Valderin's eyes were open, but only just. He gulped air through his mouth and groaned in pain.

The other guard dismounted and ran over, glancing back toward the heart of the battlefield. She crouched by her captain and rolled him on to his back. "Crossbow," she said. Her face was grim with disgust. "Wait here and stay low," she added, then darted away, zigzagging toward the source of the attack. Seconds later there was a cry.

The woman returned. "Traitors," she muttered.

Dawn placed one of her hands on Valderin's forehead and the other on his stomach beside the wound. Through the punctured chainmail she could feel the hot moisture of his blood. Valderin, who had believed in her and helped her, even defying King Eneron and the warden in the process. Dawn couldn't bear to see him like this. "He may still survive," she said, "but we have to get him back to Meridar. I don't have what I need to heal him here."

And the earthstone? said Ebony. She cocked her head to the side and clacked her beak in frustration.

I don't know, said Dawn. *I don't know.*

Valderin would die if she left him. And Princess Ona? With the guard to carry her she might just make it back to Meridar, but only if they didn't run into any more Narlaw.

Dawn looked to the south, still pressing her palms on to Valderin's wound. With every second that passed, the earthstone was slipping further and further from her grasp. And with it, all hope of defeating the Narlaw.

Horses snorted and stamped nearby, wandering aimlessly without their riders. A wind swept the meadow, flicking the stray hairs around her face. Valderin's stomach rose and fell under Dawn's hand. She felt utterly lost. Just as Valderin's life was slipping away, so was the future of Meridina. The meadows, the towns, the far off mountains. They would all be brought to ruin.

Ebony, Dawn said. *Tell me what to do.*

Ebony cawed and flapped her wings. The bond grew heavy with frustration. *The earthstone will be out of our reach soon. If we don't go after it then all this was for nothing,* she said.

Dawn nodded. She knew what she had to do, but lacked the strength of will to do it. *He'll die if I leave him*, she said instead.

Ebony grew still, the wind ruffling her feathers. She peered thoughtfully at Dawn. *He'll die if we lose the earthstone,* she said. *Everyone will, or they'll end up in the ghost-sleep.*

Dawn peered out across the flowing grasslands. *You're right,* she said. *We have to go south.* She looked at Captain Valderin. His eyelids flickered as he fought to stay conscious. Dawn knew that he wouldn't want to keep her from riding after the earthstone. She had to think for the whole kingdom.

She turned to the guard who crouched by Valderin's side. "I'll do what healing I can tonight," she said. "Then Ebony and I will go south in the morning. Ride to Meridar as fast as you can."

The guard nodded, gazing down at the captain with grim acceptance.

It's the right thing to do, said Ebony.

I know, said Dawn, but as she pressed her hand on to the wound in Valderin's side, she felt nothing but hollowness in her heart.

CHAPTER 14

Mika watched the sun rise, one hand on the reins and the other on Star's soft, sleeping back. After a long night, it seemed as if the shutters had been raised on the world. They had ridden far with barely a rest, but Mika's horse had carried her slowly and patiently north alongside Zabeh, Jen and Damon.

It felt to Mika as if the sun brought hope – that today they might find safety at last. They were close to Meridar now. A day's ride if they were lucky. The towns and villages were growing larger and closer together, and virtually all of the land had been staked out for farming. Mika had seen the scars of the passing Narlaw, too, all leading one way: east to where the demon army must be gathering.

The hooves of their four horses clopped a loose

rhythm on the road. Jen had given Mika her horse, and now rode one of the more flighty animals they had taken from the band of traitors. The horse was a comforting presence beneath Mika. As was Star.

Mika looked across at Zabeh, who seemed surprisingly alert considering how little rest they'd had.

"Do you see that?" Zabeh said. She pointed north, to where the sky still hung dark and heavy.

Mika squinted. A black shape circled there, a bird, high up as if it was hunting. But it wasn't a hunting bird.

"A raven," Mika said.

Zabeh nodded.

Mika thought of the messenger who had flown to her in Rakeen, summoning her to the council of war. In that instant, she knew there was another Whisperer near.

"We should take a look," she said, calling to Jen and Damon, who were riding ahead. "This way!" Mika led her horse through a broken gate in a tall, thorny hedgerow.

As they emerged on to a gently sloping field, Star stirred drowsily on Mika's lap. Mika was glad her companion had managed to sleep a little. Being separated from each other so violently had taken its toll on both of them. Mika could only imagine how Star must have felt as she'd been swept into the dark by the river.

Are we at the palace? Star asked.

Not quite, said Mika. She smiled and stroked Star's back and tail, scratching her gently between the ears. *But I think it's time to wake up now.*

Mika reached ahead with her senses as she and the others climbed toward the low rise at the top of the field. She felt the skittish, frightened presences of other horses. She felt people, too. And one presence – a Whisperer – so strong that she shone like a beacon in Mika's mind.

Mika nudged her horse into a trot. She was no longer afraid.

But when she crested the rise she gasped at what she saw below.

Bodies lay in the meadow. Horses stood riderless

and scared. The remains of a ruined town rose ominously beyond it all. Mika felt the taint of demons everywhere, though there were none close by. As Zabeh drew up beside her on the ridge, Mika peered down at the small group of people at the far end of the meadow. There were four soldiers, only one of whom was standing. A girl lay utterly still on the grass, a mass of blonde hair spilling over her clothes.

And there was the Whisperer.

She looked young beside the soldier-woman, staring directly at Mika, one long, dark braid of hair over her shoulder.

Mika raised a hand in greeting and the Whisperer did the same.

Please, said the Whisperer. *We need your help.*

Dawn watched the girl – Mika – as she kneeled beside the princess. She was young and still unsure of herself, which made Dawn warm to her instantly. The girl's arctic fox companion watched Dawn and Ebony curiously with her shiny black eyes and Ebony watched the fox in return.

When the girl had offered to help, Dawn had been surprised to see her go to Princess Ona first. There was nothing to be done about the princess – not yet. Valderin's health was much more urgent. If Mika could look after him, it meant Dawn and Ebony could go after the earthstone. Dawn had explained the importance of all this to Mika, who had nodded as if she understood, but she had stayed at Ona's side regardless.

Dawn glanced up at the other riders. Their journey from the highlands had obviously been a long and dangerous one. Only Mika had dismounted. The others sat, exhausted but alert, eyeing the battleground around them, no doubt expecting trouble to reappear at any moment.

Dawn felt a rush of relief. She knew these warriors could be trusted to carry Ona, Valderin and the others back to Meridar. And, hopefully, Mika could keep Valderin alive long enough for him to receive the healing he needed at the palace. But they had to set off soon.

"Mika," said Dawn, trying not to let her impatience show. "You should leave the princess. There's nothing you can do." But Mika didn't respond. "I need you to take care of the captain," Dawn persisted. "The healing rite won't last long. You have to."

Dawn, said Ebony, hunched on the flattened grass beside her. *Something's happening…*

Then Dawn felt it, too. She crouched to watch with an unspoken question on her lips.

Mika was channelling the earth, clashing with the sickness in the princess's mind. Her face contorted with furious effort.

She's attacking it, Dawn whispered to Ebony. The wind around them seemed to shift and focus in on Mika. *But it can't be done,* said Dawn. *You can't reverse the ghost-sleep. Not with the demon still walking.*

Ebony glanced up at her. *Well, she's certainly trying.*

Dawn caught the eye of one of the riders, the younger of them, a girl the same age as Mika.

The girl smiled at Dawn. "She's stronger than she looks. I was her first – she raised me from the demon's sleep."

Dawn stared, speechless.

Then she heard a gasp. She turned and saw Princess Ona, wide-eyed and awake, clutching at the patterned wool of Mika's coat.

They sat together in the long grass – Dawn, Mika and Ona. Ebony perched on Dawn's shoulder, her feathers ruffling in the persistent wind, and Star stayed close beside Mika, eyeing each member of the group with great curiosity. After the princess had recovered a little from the shock of waking, the two Whisperers had helped her away from the battleground. They had a few minutes in which to talk while the warriors prepared for the journey to Meridar.

"It was you who brought me back," said Ona, gazing at Mika with confusion and awe. Mika nodded. "Thank you." Ona clasped Mika's hand between both of hers. "And thank you for coming for me," she said to Dawn. "I didn't think…" She bowed her head. "I thought I was alone."

"You're safe now," said Dawn. Relief welled up inside her, but it was mixed with the guilt of what she could have done to stop Ona being taken in the first place. The princess looked tired and unwell. Her three days as a prisoner had changed her. But Dawn saw a new strength there, too, a toughness that gave her hope.

Mika looked slightly embarrassed, Dawn thought. She smiled at her. "It's quite a discovery you've made," she said. "Even Queen Amina was sure that the only way to wake someone was to banish the demon that attacked them."

Mika smiled shyly. "I had to try something," she said. "My best friend was in the ghost-sleep and so was my mentor."

"But how did you do it?" asked Dawn. She leaned closer to Mika.

"It's a kind of banishment, I think," said Mika. "The demon leaves a part of itself behind – a binding that traps the victim. I channel the earth and attack the binding. And when the sleeper is freed, I feel the demon leave the world. Permanently."

Dawn stared silently back at Mika.

On her shoulder, Ebony fidgeted. *What does she mean, permanently?*

I don't know, said Dawn. "You mean back to the Darklands?" she said to Mika.

Mika shook her head. The sombre look in her eyes told Dawn all she needed to know.

"The demon is gone for good?" said Dawn. "But how?"

"I don't know," said Mika. "I don't know." She looked embarrassed again. "My mentor, Astor," she said. "She was certain the demons were gone from this world completely. She felt it when I woke her."

You know what this means? said Ebony.

Dawn nodded, staring past Mika into the swaying sea of grass. "We could do what even Queen Amina failed to do," she said aloud. "We can make sure this invasion never happens again." She brought her attention back to Mika. "You have to make this work," she said. "When you reach Meridar I need you to teach the other Whisperers what you know. If I make it back with the earthstone, you can help me send the Narlaw away forever."

Mika nodded. "I'll do my best," she said.

Beside her Princess Ona looked worried. "You said *if*," she muttered. "*If* you make it back to Meridar. You have to come back. The city won't stand without you. Who will take charge? My father isn't… He's ill. He can't do it…"

Dawn met Ona's fearful gaze. "This is why I need you to help me, too," she said. "While I go after the earthstone, you'll be in charge. You have to convene the council of war, bring the Whisperers and guards together, make sure Meridar doesn't fall."

Even as she spoke, Dawn realized the terrible weight she was setting on Ona's shoulders. But Ona was a princess. The people loved her and the soldiers of Meridar would do anything for her.

"But I can't," said Ona.

"You must," said Dawn. "Like you said, the king can't lead the kingdom in this war. It's your time now. And you're stronger than you think."

Ona stared silently at the patch of flattened grass between them, and Dawn wondered if she was doing the right thing.

Before she could say more, a call went up from over by the horses. The warriors were ready.

Dawn rose to her feet and Ebony flapped gracefully into the air. The wind rushed through the grass making whispers of its own.

"It's time," said Dawn.

CHAPTER 15

The road to Meridar was quiet. Mika reached out and scanned the roadside fields and woodlands as she went, but felt nothing. The Narlaw were gathering elsewhere and the people of Meridina were already sheltering behind the walls of the capital.

Star's tail swept to and fro on the saddle. She was watching the roadside, too, and the other travellers. It was a strange group: palace guards, highland warriors, a princess and a Whisperer. And Star, of course.

Mika glanced across at the guard captain – Valderin. He was supporting himself in the saddle now, rocking gently as his deep brown horse carried him home. Mika had renewed the healing rite that Dawn had placed to stop the bleeding. In an hour she would have to renew it again. Before they parted, Dawn had instructed her to take Valderin straight to a Whisperer called Moraine when they reached the palace. She had also said that the council of war would have to go ahead without her.

Dawn, Ebony and the one uninjured palace guard had ridden south after the earthstone. Mika had never heard of such a thing before today, but Dawn's decision to pursue it said all that needed to be said about the stone's importance. Mika trusted in Dawn's knowledge, but she wasn't sure about her decision to place Princess Ona in charge in her absence.

What do think of our princess? Mika asked Star. *In Rakeen everyone said she was too mollycoddled to rule. They said the king shut her away like a precious jewel.*

I don't think she's as helpless as she looks, said Star. *But if those rumours are even half true, she won't find it easy leading a city into war.*

Mika nodded. Star's words brought to mind that the worst was yet to come. She knew that. When they reached Meridar there would be shelter and food and soldiers, but the Narlaw were close now, and they were waiting to strike. They were strong and deadly and they wanted Meridina for themselves.

Mika thought about what Dawn had asked of her: to teach the other Whisperers how to wake the victims of the ghost-sleep. She wondered how many Whisperers had gathered in Meridar and what they would think about being taught by an unknown girl from the western highlands. And what if it was a skill that couldn't be taught? Mika ran through the process of awakening in her mind. She visualized the demon binding, the particular earth trance and constant attack required to tear through the Narlaw's evil and reach the sleeper beneath. The technique was clear to her. She had performed it successfully six times already. But that didn't mean she could teach anyone else how to do it. She wasn't a mentor, she was a novice.

Mika wished Astor was there to help her. She pictured the wind shrine and the snow falling on the desolate hilltop where they had parted and her chest ached with sadness. If only she knew whether Astor was safe – if she and Suri had made it away from Rakeen and found food and shelter somewhere. She felt a sudden, fierce determination kindle inside her.

She would teach the new art of awakening in Meridar and, more importantly, she would find a way to banish the Narlaw forever. It seemed impossible – there were just so many demons – but there had to be a way, and she would do everything she could to win this war, to clear the Narlaw from the streets of Rakeen, to make the hills and valleys safe again. She would do it for Astor, wherever she was.

The afternoon wore on, cold and bright.

Ona rode, warily, behind Damon, the highland warrior who led the group. Her time with the Narlaw laid a murky, oppressive veil over every thought and feeling. She'd been imprisoned in the ghost-sleep and had returned. Now she understood the distraction her friend Yusuf had experienced in the days following his own reawakening.

The road they were following had brought them

through a patch of woodland. As Ona surveyed the trees to either side she couldn't help but remember the face of Captain Niels sneering at her, and being dragged toward the woodland inn and the dreadful people there. She looked ahead. The road rose gently for some fifty paces to the top of a low hill. She watched the highlander in front, and then beyond, to where the trees thinned at the top of the hill and opened out on to a great stretch of farmland.

And there, rising above the fields, was Meridar.

Ona's body tingled with joy and relief.

They passed between the farms and villages, and everyone they saw seemed to be travelling toward the city, its yellow stone walls and the angles of the slate roofs beyond promising safety. The Palace of the Sun, standing proudly above, promised home.

As they neared the city walls, Ona, princess of Meridina, joined the long procession of refugees. The people around her glanced nervously as she passed. Those who recognized her turned to whisper to their friends and families. Those who didn't kept a respectful distance; it was clear from her clothing and the company she kept that she was someone important, at least.

Ona walked her horse slowly amid the throng of people. At the gates the guards barked and bellowed, ushering the refugees into the city and dispensing orders: where to find food and be assigned a place to sleep; what to do with livestock and where to report for defence duties.

Ona felt trepidation rise inside her. If she did as Dawn said and took charge of the city then everyone within these walls would be reliant on her. She looked down at the refugees that surrounded her – they looked so tired and vulnerable. She couldn't do it. She didn't know how to rule a city, let alone defend one against an army of demons. Her father had never taught her how the kingdom worked. Where were the infirmaries? How many guards were there? How many horses?

As she drew closer to the gates the crowd became tighter, bodies pressed against her legs and the flanks of her horse. It was only the forward motion of the crowd that kept Ona from turning her horse around and running from the responsibility Dawn had thrust on her.

Her heart fluttered in her chest as the shadow of the city wall fell over her. A scowling, helmeted guard locked eyes with her and, after a moment of recognition, his eyes widened with shock.

"The princess!" he cried. "Make way for Princess Ona!"

The volume of the crowd increased tenfold. Heads turned and the guards cleared the way with a good deal of shouting and shoving. Then they stood to attention and saluted as she passed beneath the high stone archway.

"Welcome home, Your Highness," said the leader of the watch.

Ona nodded and thanked him. She rode uphill toward the palace, casting her gaze over the shop fronts, the warehouses and homes; the schools, taverns and infirmaries. She was suddenly excited at the thought of seeing her father. He would be so pleased to know she was safe. But how could she explain to him, the king of Meridina, that he was unfit to rule? Even considering such a thing felt like an act of betrayal. Perhaps she could stay by his side and guide him instead. She could even draw him out of his absent-mindedness – make him strong again? There had to be a way.

In four days everything had changed. She wasn't the same princess any more.

Ona peered back across the rooftops and the teeming streets – all the way to the city wall and the fields beyond. She knew one thing for sure – this was her city and she refused to let the Narlaw take it.

Dawn galloped her copper-coloured mare into the full blast of the wind – south and east, on the trail of the earthstone.

Behind her, the last woman standing from Valderin's guards rode at the same desperate, breakneck pace. Her name was Loren, and she had followed Dawn without needing to be asked.

Dawn felt Ebony high above, her companion

battling the high winds as she scanned the rolling hills and the glittering rivers for their prey.

Ebony was their eyes. And she had the scent of the demons already.

They're riding fast, she said. *We may not catch them.*

Then we'll have to ride faster, said Dawn.

She leaned lower still against the neck of her horse, who was strong, fast and agile. Dawn didn't know the horse's name, but she could feel her power and her focus. She reached out to her as she gripped the reins, letting her know that she was focused too, dead set on closing the ground with the Narlaw.

The grass whipped by and the mare thundered over the fields and leaped the meandering streams without faltering. Dawn held tight and the world flashed by. Riding like this she felt at home again, free. She was back in the Southlands, racing her friends along the rocky hillsides, whooping into the sun as her horse kicked up a long, red cloud of dust. Only now she wasn't racing for fun, she was racing for survival; for Meridina and for everyone and everything that lived there.

Ahead, she saw a river gully – three paces wide or more.

The mare leaped and sun-sparkled water flashed beneath them.

That's it! she whispered. *That's it!*

The horse galloped on and Dawn heard Loren land the jump behind her.

The wind forced tears from Dawn's eyes and her whole body ached for rest. But there could be no rest. Not until the hunt was over and she held the earthstone in her hands.

Out now!

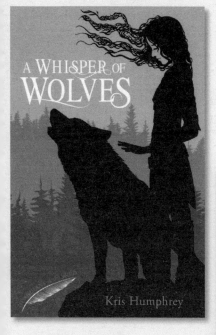

"A wonderful tale filled with enchanting characters"
Kate O'Hearn

"A powerful story set in a timeless world"
Julia Eccleshare
Lovereading4kids

A WHISPER OF WOLVES

When a raven drops a white feather at the doorstep on the day of your birth, it is a symbol of your destiny. You are a Whisperer — a guardian of the wild.

Many years have passed since the people of Meridina last knew war, but a shadow has settled over the kingdom. When Alice and her wolf companion, Storm, sense a demonic presence in the forest, they send for help to protect their village. But they're running out of time. With the entire balance of the natural world at stake, will Alice and Storm have to face the demons alone?

Read an extract…

Alice hurried through the narrow streets of Catchwood. Today was market day and the village was packed with traders from all over the mountainside; boots, hooves and cart wheels rumbled across the hard-packed mud. Alice clutched a heavy wicker basket and the jars and pots within clanked together as she wove through the market-day traffic.

She stepped aside to allow a line of mules to pass and, as she did so, she noticed an elderly man sitting beside her in the doorway of a low-ceilinged cottage, carving a chunk of wood. Alice nodded at him politely as she waited, but the man simply narrowed his eyes, casting her a look of unconcealed suspicion.

Alice turned back to the street, her cheeks burning with embarrassment and anger. She should have grown used to this by now, but her visits to the village remained as uncomfortable as ever. She tried to believe what Moraine, her mentor, had told her: that although the villagers feared her now, they would come, in time, to respect her as their Whisperer. But how long would she have to wait? She was twelve years old now and had been living here, apprenticed to Moraine, since she was old enough to walk.

She stared down at her boots and the mud stains on her long, patterned skirt – the one Moraine always insisted she wore into the village. When the last of the mules had gone by, Alice left the old man to his work, wishing she were back in the forest already.

The market square was a chaos of stalls and wagons. There were so many people – and so many animals, pulling carts or tethered to the posts and fences around the edges of the square. Colourful awnings flapped in the breeze and the stallholders bellowed their prices, vying for the custom of the crowds. Above it all stood the festival tree: a solitary pine that rose up, ancient and proud. And above the tree, the autumn sky raced with clouds.

Despite the cries of the sellers, with their ferocious bustle and salesmanship, one fact could not be hidden – most of the stalls were pitifully empty. There was simply not enough food to fill the market.

It had been a hard summer on the mountain. Edible plants had grown sparse, the streams and rivers were all but empty of fish, and those who hunted rabbit and deer were forced to travel further than ever before. In fact, the village's main hunting party had set out four days ago and not yet returned. This was the first time in years that they had missed a market day and people were beginning to talk.

Alice edged through the crowd. She hefted the wicker basket and aimed for Sal's grain stall, her first call of the day. The shadow of the festival tree slid over her and with it, like an all-powerful tide, came the smells and sounds of the traders. Alice was shoved aside by people carrying huge sacks and crates; elbows jabbed at her from every angle.

It was simply the bustle of market day – she knew this – but every nudge and push made her feel even less welcome in the village than she already did.

These errands were vital to Alice's training as a healer, but Alice knew there was more to being a Whisperer than quietly producing medicines for the villagers. There had been a time when the Whisperers were respected, and even obeyed, throughout the kingdom. Under the leadership of Queen Amina they had protected Meridina from the Narlaw and banished the demon armies back to the Darklands. Nowadays any mention of the Narlaw was greeted with a condescending shake of the head. They were little more than monsters from the history books, used for scaring children into doing their chores.

Alice wished that the demons were just ancient history, but she knew better than that. The missing hunters and the changes in the forest were small things, coincidences perhaps, but Alice felt a growing fear that something sinister was behind it all – and she knew Storm and the other wolves shared her suspicions.

She felt a pang of loneliness at the thought of Storm. But she could only ever enter the village alone. The people of Catchwood didn't understand her bond with Storm, and a fully grown wolf was not a welcome guest in any village.

She arrived at the grain stall and made her way to the front. The goods on display were meagre: half a dozen loaves, a stack of wheat-flour parcels, some salt and a single coil of dry red sausage. There would normally be four or five times as much, and an extra table of wheat and barley sacks in reserve behind the stall.

Alice waited her turn, listening in as Sal finished her conversation with another customer.

"They've been gone four days now…" said the boy. He was about Alice's age, but his face was drawn with worry. He wore the short leather apron of an apprentice blacksmith or carpenter.

"Don't you fret, Owen lad," said Sal. "I'm sure they've just gone further out, looking for a better hunting ground."

"Four days, though," said Owen. "Something has

to be wrong. Dad's never been away so long before."

Sal smiled sympathetically and the boy glanced sideways at Alice as he turned to leave.

Alice met his gaze silently. Perhaps he recognized a similar, troubled expression on Alice's face because he nodded to her solemnly before he turned and vanished into the crowds.

"The usual, is it?" Sal asked cheerily.

Alice smiled and nodded, putting the frightened eyes of the apprentice boy out of her mind. She picked two jars from her basket: one ointment for the gums and one powder to help with aching of the joints – both for Sal's elderly father. Alice liked Sal and hoped she was right about the hunters – that they had simply extended their search and would return soon with a healthy stock of meat to trade. But she couldn't help agreeing with Owen.

The tension she had noticed in the village over the past few weeks was even more obvious now. The people here were forest people, just like she was. They too would sense the change in the woods – small things, hard to pin down – as well as the lack of food and the poor hunting. To Alice it seemed as if everyone knew something terrible was looming, but nobody wished to voice their fears. It made her keener than ever to return to the forest and see what news Storm had from the wolf packs.

She added two pounds of flour and a fist of salt to her basket, thanked Sal and began pushing her way out towards her next stop. The villagers barged and jostled her, casting their sidelong looks as she passed.

Once her rounds were complete, Alice wasted no time in leaving Catchwood and the market-day crowds behind. She wove quickly towards the north gate, nodding to the guard as she passed through the wall of thick wooden stakes that surrounded the village. Immediately she felt the deep relief of being back on the wild mountainside. The breeze flowed over her, lifting her hair and catching in the folds of her skirt. The musty, human smells of the village were swept away, replaced by the sweetness of the pines and the crystalline mountain air.

Alice turned uphill towards the trees and reached out with her Whisperer sense. The tree line altered minutely as a familiar grey silhouette padded into view. Alice smiled. She ran the rest of the way, swinging the basket of supplies at her side, and plunged into the forest, letting its coolness envelop her. Dogwood and sagebrush whipped harmlessly at her legs as she ran. She ducked the low sweeping branches of oaks, and dodged between the slender aspens and pines.

And then Storm was there, grey and black and golden-eyed, nuzzling into her. Alice ran her hands through the thick, soft fur behind her companion's velvety ears. The bond between them pulsed with the warmth of their friendship – and with anticipation: Storm had something to tell her.

You've heard from the wolf packs? Alice said, her words entering Storm's mind directly. She stepped back, sensing that bad news was coming.

There's a trail, said Storm. *Lifeless forest on the high ridge – scorched earth and dead trees. It leads to the mountain pass, to the Darklands.*

Alice stared blankly off into the pines. Her heart thumped in her chest.

Narlaw, she whispered.

Yes. Storm bowed her head. *We must tell Moraine. And the elders. The village is in danger.*

Alice nodded in a state of shock. Generations had passed since the Narlaw had been banished to the Darklands. They were shape-shifters, beings who lived only to destroy the natural world. Their touch had the power to wither anything that lived. It seemed so wrong to think of such things, especially here in the great forest, with the trees swaying gently and the birds trilling their midday songs overhead.

But the wolves did not lie. And they had smelled the scent of demons.

When a raven drops a white feather at the doorstep on the day of your birth, it is a symbol of your destiny. You are a Whisperer — a guardian of the wild.

The kingdom of Meridina is under threat. When Nara and her leopard companion, Flame, receive the call to attend a Whisperers' council of war, they begin the long journey north. But signs of the shape-shifting Narlaw are everywhere. Can Nara and Flame make it to the palace or will the demons reach them first? The future of the natural world is resting on their shoulders…

ABOUT THE AUTHOR

Kris Humphrey grew up in Plymouth,
where he spent most of his time reading books,
riding around on his bike and daydreaming
about writing a book himself. Since then,
Kris has had more jobs than he cares to think
about. He has been a cinema projectionist,
a bookseller and worked at an animal sanctuary
in the Guatemalan jungle.

A Whisper of Wolves, the first book in
the Guardians of the Wild series,
was Kris's first novel.